MURDER IN PROSPECT

— AN EVE SAWYER MYSTERY —

MURDER IN PROSPECT

— AN EVE SAWYER MYSTERY —

JANE SUEN

Murder in Prospect: An Eve Sawyer Mystery

Jane Suen books are available for order through Ingram Press Catalogues.

www.janesuen.com

Printed in the United States of America

First Printing: August 2024

Ebook ISBN: 978-1-951002-33-6

Paperback ISBN: 978-1-951002-34-3

Audiobook ISBN: 978-1-951002-35-0

In memory of Grover, a sweet, troublemaking little beagle.

PROLOGUE 1

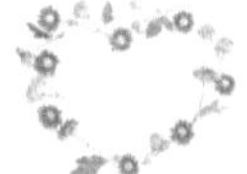

HE LOVED ALL OF HER. FROM THE TOP OF HER HEAD, long golden locks tumbled past her slender neck and across exquisitely rounded shoulders. Her petite frame tapered at the trim waist, then widened to accommodate bony hips attached to shapely legs, slim ankles, and dainty feet. But it was her hazel eyes that melted his heart—the gateway to her soul that she'd opened up to him. He could go there, to the place that was his, and hers—theirs.

He remembered the scent of fresh rain and roses and sassafras that was uniquely hers. He could smell it now, his nose buried in the soft skin of her graceful neck, inhaling her fragrance.

She had asked him if he loved her, shining eyes trusting and sparkling, yet fragile and childlike. They had kissed, and she drew her head back, looking straight into his eyes for his answer. Every cell in his body wanted to scream his love. Yet something held him back. It wasn't so simple. To promise that was to give his eternal vow. A voice whispered inside his head. He'd have to live with the guilt.

He glimpsed the flicker of pain and disappointment in her expressive eyes before her eyelids dropped. The moment was gone. He knew instinctively he'd made a fatal mistake, one that hurt to the depths of her soul.

He reached out, but it was too late. She had twirled around and dashed out the door.

It was a few days later that the mailman delivered her letter. It was dated that day—the last time they'd meet.

PROLOGUE 2

THE MAN HAD SCOUTED THE LOCATION AND PARKED HIS reliable old diesel down the street from the house, where he could watch the front door and wait. For the fifth day in a row, like clockwork, the door opened right on schedule and a figure in a long-sleeved top and loose pants exited the house to jog down the driveway past a parked car, before turning left onto the street away from him.

He stepped out of his car, hair tucked under a cap, wearing a black zip-up hoodie and dark jeans. Closing the car door quietly while he took out a pocket knife, he walked calmly toward the vehicle in the driveway.

The man stood still and scanned the area, then crouched down on the paved ground and slid under the car. He worked quickly, finding the brake line, and nicked the brake hose, not severing it—just enough for the brake fluid to trickle out.

He left before the jogger got back.

CHAPTER ONE

I had thirty minutes between classes today. Enough time for a quick break. I stopped at the student center, which was on my travel path to my next class. I zoomed across the atrium, straight to the new coffee shop where they made delicious hot chocolate with an espresso machine. I couldn't get enough of it, even though I was a coffee kind of girl.

I had it timed down to a science. It was my routine now—a middle-of-the-week treat.

"Hey, Eve," a man's deep voice called out from behind me.

I turned around with a smile, recognizing the familiar voice and the face to go with it. "Hi, Bob," I said, "how's it going?" I had seen little of Bob Harding this semester, and we didn't have any classes together. Cassie had invited him to house-sit with the three of us —her, Randall, and I—at her aunt's house over the Christmas holiday, but Bob had plans already and politely declined. I'd been meaning to catch up with him, but I got busy with school and dropped the ball.

"You got a minute?" he asked.

This man didn't waste words. But there was something different about him. I sensed a somberness and a weight that pushed his voice even deeper.

"Your hot chocolate is ready," said the barista at the register.

I grabbed my drink and dropped a tip in the jar.

"I have about twenty-five minutes. We can sit and talk," I said.

Bob nodded as I took my cup and headed to a small table tucked in a corner. I wondered why he was all serious and what was on his mind. Bob was the guy who everyone thought of as solid, dependable, and certainly not the kind that rushed to judgement. He didn't wear his feelings on his sleeve and kept his emotions in check—this tall and dark-haired man, with a deep voice to match.

I remembered how steady, calm, and reassuring he was when we worked together on cases at Lolly Beach and around Route 82. He kept his cool. Even when there was murder. But something was off today. The somber look on his face brought a feeling of unease over me. He'd dealt with life-and-death situations, and he was the rock for all of us. I just couldn't imagine anything or anyone throwing Bob off his tracks. This had to be a big deal for him.

I watched him move toward me. Even his walk was slightly unsteady, as if each stride wasn't perfectly in sync. He walked slower, too. And when he sat down across the table, the frown on his forehead deepened.

"Been busy?" I asked lightly.

He shook his head, as if that wasn't it. Bob kept his eyes down, staring at the container cupped between his hands, the steam curling and rising.

"I sometimes get coffee," I said, filling the silent lull. "I'm into their hot chocolate now. Gotta try it if you haven't." I ended my sentence lamely. Hoping he'd tell me. I knew it wouldn't do any good to push him too hard. It never worked with Bob. He'd talk when he was good and ready. And he seemed almost ready just then. Had he changed his mind? What was so important a few minutes ago that he wanted to talk to me? I reached out and nudged his arm. It was the only thing I could think to do. If he wanted to talk, I was here and ready.

He looked up and sighed. "You know why I didn't spend winter break with you guys?"

I shook my head, thinking about the house-sitting we did at Fools Lane and the man hanging from the tree. "Yeah, you said you couldn't make it because you had plans already."

"Yes, that's right." He ran his thumb around the cup's rim, pausing for a moment. "I went home to see my uncle Will."

I held my breath and waited for more. I knew Bob's uncle had raised him after his parents died.

"He ... he invited me back home to spend the holidays."

"Did you have a good Christmas?"

"We had a quiet celebration at home—just the two of us. We'd agreed on no gifts."

"You spent *time* with your uncle. You gave him the gift of time, which is more precious than wrapped presents."

He nodded. But he was holding something back.

"But you wanted to talk to me about something else?"

"No, I mean ... *yes*." He squeezed his eyes. "It's about my uncle. He, uh ... he wasn't his old self."

Words weren't exactly flowing. Whatever was bothering him was stuck inside, and I was determined to pull it out gently. Why wasn't he talking? We'd been friends and had faced danger together and seen death in front of us. I couldn't just leave him like this, even if it meant skipping my next class. Bob wasn't just anyone. I watched as he took another sip of his coffee. Yes, I'd give him all the time he needed. He'd been there for me. We had each other's backs.

"So, what's this about your uncle?"

"My uncle is dead."

I heard the words uttered abruptly, enunciated with finality. Questions immediately ran through my mind. I didn't know how old Will was. Was he close to Bob's father's age? Or much younger or older? How did he die?

I managed to say, "I'm so sorry," holding back those questions on the tip of my tongue. I didn't want to pry, as Bob was private about personal matters and rarely spoke of his family. I knew he had been a child when his parents passed, and he had no siblings. Maybe that had something to do with it.

He didn't speak, letting the emptiness fill the air.

"Was it during Christmas—when you were there?"

"No, it was after the holidays."

"After you came back to school?" I whispered.

He gave a slight nod. "And that's the last time I saw him—during winter break."

"Was there a memorial service?"

"No. He always said he didn't want one. Just get him a decent burial."

"Did you attend?"

"Yes. I went home on Friday and flew back. The burial was on Saturday. I left right after that." His eyes teared up.

"I'm sorry for your loss," I whispered.

I thought back to the tragic death of Mead Parker during the winter break. Cassie, Randall, and I had found him hanging from a tree in the backyard of the house where we were staying. Bob had been spared that tragedy. Little did I know he would be dealing with a death in his family, someone close to him and his father figure. Maybe he thought he could share it with me now, since we had been involved in murder cases. Maybe he trusted me since we were friends. If talking about it helped, that was the least I could do. Death was the hardest for the living.

"Eve, I have to go back."

I cocked my head. "Go back, when?"

"Spring break starts next week, on Saturday."

"To pay your respects at the grave?"

"There's something else I have to do."

I sensed he struggled with something else. "And that's it?"

"I ... don't know, yet."

"Well, we'll be on break an entire week, plus the Saturday before and the Sunday after. That's nine days."

"I'm leaving Friday afternoon, after my morning exam." He paused to look me in the eye.

I hitched a breath, seeing his intensity and urgency. He was deadly serious. "You need my help," I said.

"Come with me to Colorado, please."

"I don't understand what's going on. How can I help you?"

"I can't put my finger on it, but something doesn't feel right. I need you to look into this. Find out what's going on."

"Do you have anything concrete?"

"No," he said. "No proof. Not yet."

Bob was a friend in need. And he was in grief and had lost the only family he had left. I did a quick check of my schedule for next week. My last exam was on Thursday afternoon.

"I'm free ... but Mom has been expecting me to go home and see her on spring break. I need to call her first." I pulled out my phone and held up the palm of my hand like *hold on*, as I stood up and moved away to find a quiet spot to talk.

Mom answered on the first ring. I told her about Bob's invite, and she asked me if I wanted to go. I was torn between helping him and wanting to make up for the time I was away at Fools Lane over the winter break. She brought up my sleuthing skills in solving murder cases and that she knew I couldn't say no to someone's cry for help. Mom and I discussed this before a decision was made.

The call finished, I walked back to our table. Bob stared at me like he was anxious and waiting.

"I'm coming with you."

He slumped and sighed in relief, and then smiled like I had just delivered the best news. "Good, I'll book the plane and get us two tickets to fly out on Friday afternoon."

"Okay."

"I'll text you the flight information," Bob said. "And come by and pick you up."

"I'll be ready."

CHAPTER TWO

I was excited about the trip. I looked at a map and checked the distance. But a part of me was anxious about flying. It would be my first time on an airplane.

I was afraid of heights.

Truth be told, being on a plane rising to higher altitudes to fly over the Rocky Mountains in Colorado stoked my fears. It was different than reading about it in textbooks. I remembered learning about the Rockies and the famous Pikes Peak in grade school. The teacher told us the mountain was the tallest there and people from all over the world went to see it. It was the inspiration for the words of a poem, which became the song "America the Beautiful." I told myself I'd have to see this famous symbol of Americana if I ever got to Colorado.

It didn't bother me to travel on short notice. After my exam on Thursday, I packed light. One suitcase. A few changes of clothes, including jeans and tops, underwear, and socks. One black dress and a jacket. Toiletries, a hairbrush, and my laptop.

Bob had texted me the flights. We planned to leave two hours before. He'd packed the day prior. All he had to do after his exam was to pick me up and we'd be on our way.

When Bob showed up in his pickup, I was ready to go. I hopped in on the passenger side and belted in the seat. He took one look at me and paused, the vehicle still in park. "You okay?" he asked.

He was perceptive about this sort of thing. My fears. He'd found out about my fear of snakes when we worked on a case off Route 82. I must have given off similar vibes.

I gulped. No use trying to hide it. "Fear of flying," I said, quickly adding, "This is my first time."

"I remember my first," he said softly. "I was nervous."

I rubbed my sweaty palms on my jeans. I hoped he didn't notice or regret inviting me.

"You won't be alone. I'll be there," he said. "Remember how you overcame your fear of snakes?"

He kept his eyes on me. Steady.

It was coming back to me now.

The fear had become more than a figment of my imagination. It gripped me in my dreams and during the day. The fear had grown in my mind to some inflated size and held me captive. I pressed my lips together, ready to tackle the fear of flying. I knew I wasn't the first and wouldn't be the last. I had to face it full on.

CHAPTER THREE

THE PILOT ANNOUNCED THE APPROACH TO DENVER airport, and the flight attendants prepared for landing. I sat in a window seat during the flight, Bob next to me in the two-seat row. I had witnessed the marvels of man's aviation technology and soared high in the sky. My nerves had gradually calmed as the plane reached cruising altitude and activities resumed: muted conversations and occasional laughter, flight attendants serving beverages, passengers tearing or ripping pretzel bags open, the quieter unclasping of seat belts, and the opening and closing of the overhead storage bins.

As I became more accustomed to flying, my anxiety subsided, firm in the knowledge of having experienced my inaugural flight, miles above the Earth. I smiled at Bob, and he acknowledged it. I pulled up my seat and secured my seat belt for the descent to Denver.

After landing, we made our way through the airport toward the rental car counter.

"I'll get us a vehicle," Bob said.

"Okay."

While he signed the paperwork and made the payment, I strolled to the end of the counter to check out the information on a display rack. I picked up a map and some brochures and travel and sightseeing guides for visitors. I glanced his way as he held up the paperwork and waved me over. We left the airport and went straight to the rental parking lot area, since each of us had only one piece of carry-on luggage and didn't need to go to baggage claim.

I caught my first sight of Colorado and felt a rush of excitement when we walked outside the building, and my heart beat faster in anticipation of the unknown adventure that lay ahead. I took a deep breath, filling my lungs with the fresh air.

"I made it through!"

"The trip wasn't so bad, was it?" Bob asked.

I smiled. "No, it was nothing like my wild imagination."

"Ready for a drive?" He gestured to our rental, a small white sedan, economical in gas and in price.

"Let's go."

Bob got in the driver side and adjusted his seat and checked out the car's controls.

"Where are we headed?"

"Prospect. It's a small town about an hour away." He turned, eyes glinting. "If you've never been out west, this'll be a real treat. It was once a booming gold-mining town. Got a new life as a historic town."

"Really? Wow! Is it just like the Wild West in the westerns on TV?" I asked, giddy like a child.

He laughed. "You'll see."

CHAPTER FOUR

I pulled up the zipper of my jacket. Coming from the South, the change in weather was noticeable. Luckily, Bob had warned me ahead of time how to pack and bring a warm jacket. I shivered partly because of excitement as Bob drove.

"Look, the rocks and soil are red here," I said, gazing out the window. The sun was out, casting its rays over the countryside. The reddish rocky landscape was a contrast to the familiar verdant greens of the Southern hills.

"That's why they call it Red Rocks."

I rolled down the window to take in the view.

The scenery that flashed by conveyed the harshness of the land out in the elements, exposed to the blowing wind and storms, left to the mercy of the weather. Barren lands and rough terrain that withstood changing seasons. The snow had melted. In the change, a quietness covered the area, undisturbed through the winter's rest.

"It's breathtakingly beautiful in the summer," Bob said. He smiled. "You should see it then."

My mind pictured the countryside with gorgeous wildflowers and a soft breath of wind. And horses galloping frcc as they ran. Wild and undomesticated, living among the other creatures of this vast land. There was so much to see here. I swallowed, taken aback by the beauty of it all.

I closed my eyes and let the sun warm my face. It was a world away from home, this place where I'd never been.

CHAPTER FIVE

Bob filled me in a bit about his uncle during the ride.

"What do you call him?"

"I just called him Uncle Will. His full name was William Harding."

"What was he like?"

"He was smart. Worked hard. Didn't believe in vacations. Said it was a waste of time."

"So was he a grumpy old man?"

Bob didn't answer right away. "I have faint memories of my early years. He was different then."

"Different … how so?"

"Well, he laughed more—a lot, in fact. It was fun to be around him then."

"And later?"

"Later, he was a changed man, like darkness had snuffed the light out."

"Like depression?"

He paused, shaking his head. "No, it wasn't quite like that."

"I don't understand."

"It's hard to explain. There was sadness, but also something else that brought darkness. And it wasn't like one day it was sunny, and the next day it rained, and the next day it was sunny again."

"Hmm, it sounds more perpetual, like he couldn't shake it off."

"We were all going through this mourning period after my parents died. But my uncle took it especially hard. I was dealing with emotional issues and couldn't see beyond my own self. It took a while before I realized he'd changed."

"Was he close to your father?"

"Yes, my father was the firstborn, and about a year later my uncle was born."

"Did he look up to his big brother?"

"According to my father, he couldn't shake his shadow. Uncle Will followed him around and wanted to do whatever he did."

"It must have hit him hard."

"Yes, hard enough to have changed him."

"Did he ever marry? Have kids?"

"Naw. Maybe it was because of me, having to take care of me and making me his focus."

"The loss—the double loss—pulled you two closer," I said.

"We held on to each other. It was just the two of us left in our family."

"How did he do as a parent?"

Bob thought it over. "We were a family unit, like it or not."

"The car accident," I said. "Did you two ever talk about it?"

He shook his head quickly and emphatically. "Never. He never brought it up, and I avoided it. Period. It was too painful to think about it, much less talk about it."

"You'd spare his pain, and vice versa. Do you think you have closure?"

"It doesn't feel that way. It's like I have a piece of food caught in my throat and it's stuck. I missed my parents terribly, and I had nobody to talk to, so I bottled it inside. Told myself I had to be brave, and that I didn't need to upset my uncle."

It was like the dam had broken and words spilled out. I had never seen Bob this way before.

Maybe it was the environment. Away from college, here in the beauty of the Wild West, amongst the red rocks and hills, miles from the airport. This was home for Bob, where his roots were. As we sped down the highway, the anticipation of the unknown beckoned to me. The thousands of miles traveled bringing us closer to the destination. And perhaps to the heart of Bob's unease.

CHAPTER SIX

The road sign marked the miles to the town. I glanced at the odometer and calculated how long it'd take us to get there. The highway was clear. We were the only vehicle on the road for about the last twenty minutes, after having passed an ancient pickup truck. We were getting close.

"There's Prospect," Bob said, reading a dusty sign. "Population one thousand two hundred forty-one."

I wondered about the age of the sign and whether they had gained or lost people since it was erected. "Who would change the numbers and how often are they updated? Would they replace the sign just to update the population count?"

"I don't know. It was a mining town founded in the mid-1800s during the gold rush," Bob said. "It became a boomtown then. The place almost went bust after the gold ran out. Now it's a historic mining town that's popular with tourists."

We passed a gas station on the outskirts of town. Main Street was an eyeful of colorful wooden buildings lining the road from one end to the other. It was almost like time had stopped. Most of the buildings preserved the history.

Bob pointed out an old-timey general store, a saloon or inn, a post office that had also been a Western Union or telegram office, a bank, a feed store, a sheriff's office and jail, a hardware store, and a doctor's office. A few buildings had hitching posts in front. I could imagine the horses tied to them.

I looked around at the painted storefronts, some with signs reminiscent of what it once was. Like the merchandise store. Like Prospect Inn, which may have been a saloon once with rooms to rent. Or perhaps it had been a boardinghouse.

Bob pulled in front of the inn and parked. I wondered if it was the only place to stay in town, as we hadn't passed a motel yet.

I got out and stretched.

"We're staying here?" I asked.

"Yes, it's my uncle's place."

"*This* was his home?"

"Him and a few guest boarders," Bob said. "It's how he made his living."

We got out of the car and grabbed our luggage.

"Come, I'll show you around."

I followed him up the porch to the front door. A crooked wooden Welcome sign with an arrow pointed the way.

Bob punched in the front door code and opened it. We entered the foyer. The front room housed a reception area, which comprised a table with another Welcome sign, a basket with envelopes, and a guest book. I didn't see anyone there to greet us.

He looked in the basket and picked up two envelopes with his name on both. "Our rooms are ready," Bob said, as he opened the envelopes and pulled out two keys.

He turned to me. "Room two or three?"

"Doesn't matter." I shrugged.

"They're across from each other." He held up the keys.

I reached for the closest one. "Two is good."

He gestured toward the stairs. "Let's go up and get rid of our bags. Then I'll give you a tour of the rest of the house."

The stairs were worn and they creaked as we went up to the second floor. The railings appeared to be flimsy. I wondered if they were up to modern code. Probably not. But I figured they were likely more authentic, like the original.

Doors lined the upstairs hallway on both sides. A modern closet door, painted bright white, closed off the room closest to the stairs. Probably a storage area, I thought.

Bob followed my gaze. "We installed a washer and dryer, and a linen closet with storage space here. Easier for the housekeeper rather than lugging all the laundry and supplies up and down the steps."

"That's a smart upgrade," I said.

Room two was the second door on our right. I pulled my key out and unlocked it, hearing the click. The room was larger than I'd expected. Maybe because it was square rather than the narrow rectangular rooms in motels. This was like the size of a bedroom in an older home. It was simply and tastefully decorated. A bed, a wooden chest of drawers, a nightstand with a lamp, and a small table with two chairs.

There were two closed doors in the room. I opened the first one, peeked in, and saw it was a cramped bathroom. A toilet, an itty-bitty sink, and a shower. I half expected a tub in the center of the room, like I'd seen in the movies. The second door opened to a narrow closet with a few hangers and a shelf on top stacked with extra blankets.

"It gets cold up here," Bob said.

I looked around for a fireplace.

He seemed to read my mind. "Fire hazard. No wood burning."

"I'm good with that. And electric lights." I glanced at the overhead lights and the fixtures, and looked out the window, which was the only source of natural light. It was a divided wood window with small panes of glass. A cloth curtain served as the window shade. No blinds.

"It's more authentic." Bob grinned.

"Nice carpet," I said, observing the thick plush rug under the bed, over the wood floor.

"That's solid wooden flooring that was restored and refinished."

"It's beautiful," I said, admiring it. "Is it the original?"

"Yes," he said. "Some of the boards were in pretty bad shape though."

I set my luggage down and sat on the bed, bouncing on the mattress. It was harder than I was used to, but to my relief, it wasn't too soft, which would have been worse.

Bob turned to go.

I jumped up from the bed, followed him out to his room across the hall, and took a look. It was just like mine. I wondered how thick the walls were and how good the plumbing was in this old house.

Bob gestured toward the hallway. "The other rooms are like these."

"Which room was your uncle's?"

"It's downstairs. You want to see it?"

"Yes, please."

Bob paused at the bottom of the stairs and pointed to the right side of the house. "There's a small library, the dining room, and the kitchen. They occupy a larger space than his living area and the office."

It turned out that Uncle Will had a suite. Across from the reception area, there was a door on the left side of the house. It was his office. Another door led to his bedroom and adjoining bathroom.

I peeked in his office as Bob opened the door and caught a faint whiff of something that was like a mixture of dirt, old books, tobacco, and musty odor. It apparently hadn't been aired for a long while.

Walls lined with books filled one side of the room. Sunlight filtered in from the window through partly drawn semi-sheer curtains, brightening an expansive mahogany desk. Pens and paper clips were scattered across the desk. It was cleared on one end, a pile of stacked papers and stuff pushed aside.

A tied shoebox on the smooth dark surface caught my attention, and I could see Bob's name on top of the lid, handwritten in black ink.

"Bob," I whispered.

He made his way toward the desk, touching it, running his fingers along the wood reverently before he sat in the chair and pulled the cord on the solitary lamp, which cast warm soft light in the room.

Bob didn't open the box right away. His fingers traced the writing of his name, caressing it. He appeared lost in his thoughts, as if going over memories. He was in his own world, transported to another time, maybe with a hint of sadness and yet comfort in the familiar.

I held my breath. It felt sacred to be here in the intimacy of the small office, where a man had left impressions of himself. A well-used desk and a worn chair, cold and abandoned. I felt like a stranger intruding, although invited.

"Your uncle's handwriting?" I didn't have to ask. I coughed politely, took a step back, and waved in the direction of the closed door. "Uh, I'll leave you to it. Why don't I come back later?"

Bob didn't argue—he looked up and gave a slight nod as he lifted the lid off the shoebox.

CHAPTER SEVEN

I TURNED AROUND AND MADE A HASTY RETREAT, grabbing the doorknob and opening it.

I came face to face with a woman dressed in a plain gray dress. She looked as surprised as I was. She was older than me, in her forties or fifties, I estimated. She quickly recovered and cranked her neck to look over my shoulder. The woman was taller than me, and there was no way I could've blocked her view otherwise. I waited for some apology or something. There was none forthcoming. I wondered if she could be the maid —or the maid-in-charge would be more fitting.

"Who are you?" she asked point-blank.

I was taken aback by the unpleasant tone of her voice. Sharp, demanding. I heard suspicion and irritation, too.

"Ma'am," I said politely, "my name is Eve Sawyer." I held up my room key.

I had the feeling she already knew that. Her face

registered no surprise.

"And what is your name?" I kept my voice low and as friendly as possible.

She didn't reciprocate. She brushed me aside and rushed past me, marching straight up to Bob.

"You didn't let me know you're here," she said accusingly.

I imagined her eyes glaring, shooting darts at him, even though her back was turned to me. I stepped back into the room. I wasn't going to leave her alone with Bob and I wanted to know who she was and what right she had to act this way.

He looked up, one hand frozen as it clutched the lid of the box. "Oh, Mrs. Bell." Bob looked at me and then back to her. "I see you met Eve." He remained calm and casual. Maybe he was trying to defuse the situation. I imagined her lips to be pursed, clamped together tighter than a clam shell.

"You really shouldn't be here," she said.

"I have every right to be here."

"That remains to be seen," she snapped, before turning around on her heels.

Bob dropped the lid back on the shoebox, picked it up, tucked it under his arm, and stood up. "Don't mind Scarlett." He walked around the desk toward me. "Now what was I saying? Would you like to continue the tour?"

"Where to?"

"How about the dining room?"

I nodded enthusiastically.

CHAPTER EIGHT

The dining room had a large table occupying the center of the room. A pantry with dishes stood at the far corner. On top of a waist-high cabinet alongside the wall was a coffee station with a pot of coffee, clean mugs turned upside down on a tray, a hot water carafe, and a ceramic sugar bowl and creamer set. Mini coffee spoons were on a plate. Square folded napkins lined up next to the spoons, the folded edges arranged in a pretty spread.

The room was quiet. Empty.

I pulled Bob back toward the table. "I need to know. Tell me what's going on," I said firmly, meeting his gaze.

He sighed, shoulders slumped, appearing resigned. Then he turned around and headed upstairs.

I followed him as he climbed the steps and stopped in front of his room, key in his hand, poised at the keyhole. I waited, allowing him the space and time he needed.

He opened his door and hesitated, then pushed it wide open and gestured for me to come in.

I wasted no time claiming one seat by the small table, nudging the other chair toward Bob.

"You know I'm not one to talk about my family," he said, sitting down and setting the shoebox carefully on the table.

I merely tipped my head.

"I couldn't …" His voice cracked, but he continued. "My parents … it was too painful … it's still painful."

"I'm sorry," I said. I truly didn't know, although I'd sensed a darkness and immense sadness. Part of me wanted to pull away. I didn't want to go there. But now he was going there, facing his fear and pain and hurt.

"I was young then, when the car accident happened." He shook his head slowly. "I was old enough to know what happened. I remember being taken out of school that day and the rest of the week. But I was too young to under-stand … to really understand even the meaning of death."

I felt a dampness on my cheek and wiped my tears away.

"No child should ever have to deal with death." He gritted his teeth. "So I kept it inside, went back to school, and went on with my life."

"Your uncle raised you."

"Yes, he brought me out here. I think it was to get away from what happened. And … for himself too."

"The two of you mourned together," I mumbled. "You didn't have anyone else?"

"No other family. My uncle was single then and now."

"You must have been very close."

"I always liked him, when my parents took me to see him." His voice became hoarse. "But I never imagined my parents would die and I'd end up living here."

"You were just a child."

"But why did it have to happen?" he said, his face twisted with agony. "Was it something I did?"

Maybe guilt also weighed heavily on him. I gripped his hand tightly. "Don't blame yourself. You were just a child and you had nothing to do with it."

Tears flooded his eyes and streamed down his face. Bob's shoulders shook as he sobbed his heart out. It came from deep within. Letting go, releasing what he had held inside for so long.

I reached out and hugged him for an indeterminate time. I wasn't counting.

CHAPTER NINE

Bob had emptied his tears and washed his face. A noise out in the hallway interrupted our peace. He jumped up and opened his door in time to see a girl run past. Scarlett Bell was chasing her and shouting. They reached the end of the hallway, and the girl turned around. We had a clear view of her frightened face. Scarlett towered over the girl, her hand raised, gripping a wooden spoon.

Bob crossed the distance with running strides. He came up behind and caught her wrist in midair. Scarlett wrestled him and shook her arm in an attempt to get free.

I took this opportunity to snatch the spoon away. The girl straightened up, pressing her back against the wall. She had something clutched in her hand. Her head swiveled as she looked frantically left and right. In an instant, she dashed between us and escaped down the hallway toward the stairs.

I ran after her, while Bob stayed with Scarlett. The girl flew down the stairs to the first floor, and out the door. I didn't think twice about stopping to put my jacket on when a gust of wind blew. I followed her outside. She glanced back to see if I was still there, then spurred on with renewed energy.

I wasted no time racing after her down the sidewalk, past a row of storefronts. When she reached the intersection, the light had turned red, and she took the crosswalk to the other side. I was right behind her, taking advantage of the light change too.

The sunshine played on her hair, which had come loose, the long strands waving in the breeze, undulating with each step. She ran in a zigzag line, darting this way and that to avoid obstacles. I didn't think she was lost—it would be absurd to get lost on Main Street in this small town. I was in pretty good shape, but out of breath. Maybe it was because the air was thinner here.

I had a surge of energy and caught up, blocking her against the wall of a corner store. My chest heaving and short of breath, I managed to say, "Please ... I just want to talk to you."

It was her luminous eyes—soft, scared, doe-like—that spoke to me. "I just want to talk," I repeated. "I'm not going to hurt you, okay?" I stepped back gradually as I held her gaze. She stayed still, except for rasping breaths.

"Do you understand me?" I asked.

She nodded.

"What is your name?"

Her lips parted, then she licked them.

"Look, my name is Eve Sawyer. I'm a friend of Bob's." I pointed back toward the inn.

Bob had been a thousand miles away. Maybe she'd never met him.

I tried again. "Okay." I gestured toward the inn again. "Upstairs with me—he's Will's nephew. He's been away at school at Midway College. I also go to school there and I'm a friend of his." I paused. "Bob. Do you know him?"

She nodded slowly.

I managed a smile to put her at ease. "So tell me your name."

"Serena." The answer came soft and clear.

"Are you okay?"

She didn't respond.

"Tell me why you were at the inn. Why was she shouting at you?"

"I ... I messed up."

I looked down at her clenched hand. "You took something that doesn't belong to you?"

She shook her head vigorously. I felt she was telling the truth. Even at this age, I saw something like stubbornness and a bit of hurt that I had questioned her integrity.

"What do you have in your hand?" I asked gently.

"A bracelet."

"Is it yours?"

"Yes, it's mine." She spat out the words. "She gave it to me last year."

"Why would she do that?"

"She was drunk that night."

"I don't understand. Why?"

"Because I had worked for her, and she promised to pay me in cash. But she didn't have any money. Blew it all on drink."

"So she paid you with the bracelet instead?"

"Yes."

"You didn't demand cash?"

She threw her head back and laughed hysterically. "Are you kidding? She's my mother!"

CHAPTER TEN

Bob was in his room when I got back to the inn, the contents of the shoebox dumped out on the table.

"You find anything interesting?"

He held up a small blue toy car. "My uncle gave me this on my seventh birthday. I played with it for years." He rubbed his fingers over the dull surface, tracing its familiar shape. His eyes glazed, reliving the memories again, taking him back over the years. "I thought I'd lost it. After I left."

I leaned over to look at the other items, which were clearly other mementos that his uncle had saved. Will was a sentimental man.

A math test, the numbers written in a child's handwriting, and the name "Bob." At the top of the paper was a bold "A" written in red letters, and next to it a "94" grade.

Bob grinned. "He helped me with my homework."

"What's that?" I pointed to a few papers folded

twice, in half and again, into card size. They were held together by a paper clip.

He slipped off the clip and opened them. One had a big heart-shaped drawing in red, and the words "I love you" scrawled in crayon. Another was a "Merry Christmas" card with a drawing of a fir tree and presents under it—and an arrow pointing to a bow-tied box with Bob's name on it. There was also a stick drawing of a man and child.

Under the drawings was a hardback book, a picture of a huge red dog on the cover. I smiled, remembering how I enjoyed listening to my mother read this book to me at bedtime. I had pleaded with her to buy it. Having settled my gaze on the red dog, I'd become obsessed with bringing it home with me. If I couldn't have a real live dog, this was my choice. My mother had gone back to the bookstore and bought several more, and we rotated these books, reading one story each night. I fixated on Clifford the Big Red Dog until I outgrew the books. Even then, I'd occasionally read one again with a smile plastered on my face. I let this memory play in my mind. It was a keeper.

"He kept these for me," Bob whispered, as he picked up a framed photo of a smiling youngster and a handsome older man. "That's Uncle Will and me."

I leaned close, studying the snapshot of the little boy gazing adoringly at the man, who wore a proud smile, his arm wrapped around the boy's shoulder. The camera had caught them in a happy moment, capturing a forever memory. It was a candid shot, not a posed photo. I lingered on it before switching my gaze to Bob's face. My heart ached, looking at the way his head drooped and his body sagged. Part of me wanted to meet this man who earned the adoration of a child, although I knew it could never happen.

CHAPTER ELEVEN

I woke up in the morning in a strange bed. I had slept well. Maybe it was the bed, the hefty mattress, and the fluffy pillows on a solid wood frame. Maybe it was the place, a certain atmosphere of a quiet small town surrounded by nature, far from the rush-hour traffic of busy city streets.

Maybe I was exhausted from the trip to Colorado—the anticipation of my first flight, and the excitement mixed with fear as we boarded the airplane. Bob had comforted me, his voice soothing as I gripped his arm, panicking from the thunderous roar and the vibrations rattling the plane as it gathered speed, took off, and ascended. I was more at ease when the plane made the descent, although I closed my eyes in the final approach, praying for a safe landing amid the jolts, shuddering, and bumps.

I thought more about Bob. He'd opened up to me. About his family. The death of his parents. His uncle

Will who raised him. And with his recent death, grief still traumatized Bob, so fresh and raw. The photo I saw showed a man in his prime. Strong, healthy, and happy. His death had to be premature. I estimated he was in his thirties then, or maybe early forties, which would have put him in his fifties now. Too young to die. Bob had alluded to a worry, and that something wasn't right. I hadn't pried. I could try to second-guess what was still bothering him, or I could be patient.

A knock on the door interrupted my thoughts, catching me by surprise.

"Hey, are you up?"

It was Bob. I yawned. "What time is it?" I called out from the comfort of my bed.

"Time for breakfast, sleepyhead. Get downstairs."

"Okay, meet you there." I scuttled to find my clothes, tugging on a long-sleeve cotton shirt and a pair of faded blue jeans. I checked my hair in the bathroom mirror and brushed my teeth for about thirty seconds, then opened the door and hurried down the stairs.

I caught the smell of bacon and my ears picked up the sizzle in the frying pan emanating from the kitchen. I'd stopped eating meat for years, but some primal element in my brain still reacted to the aroma of bacon. I'd read somewhere that bacon was the hardest and the last thing for a meat-eater to give up. But when I quit eating meat, it was by choice, and I stuck with it.

"How about some scrambled eggs?" Bob said, slipping two pats of butter in a small frying pan as he whipped fluffy eggs in a bowl.

"Yum. What can I do?"

"There are avocados in the fridge if you want to slice one up."

I smiled, not wasting any time. "Perfect."

"And orange juice," he said. "And I've made a fresh pot of coffee."

I glanced at the clock on the wall and realized I'd overslept. My cheeks flushed.

Bob noticed. "Hey, the jet lag will do that to you."

"Thanks for letting me sleep."

"You picked a good time. We had a small group for breakfast, and they've cleared out. The kitchen is all ours now."

We worked together quickly. He cooked while I set the table and got the drinks. My plated eggs and avocado slices painted a pretty picture next to the OJ and the coffee. After we sat, I chowed down on my food with relish.

I finished eating first and leaned back in my chair, thinking about a second cup of coffee.

"You up for adventure today?" Bob asked.

"Where to?"

He didn't explain, saying instead, "But first I've got a quick meeting with the attorney who's the executor for my uncle's estate."

"Oh, aren't you the executor?"

"No, my uncle had made arrangements. He wanted

me to concentrate on my studies, so he gave that job to James Garrett."

"He didn't want you to be burdened."

"Uncle Will had been planning his affairs for a while. I came back over the winter break to see him. That's why I couldn't go with you to house-sit over the holidays."

"I knew you had plans."

"He asked me to come home. At the time I wondered if everything was okay."

"Was he ill?"

Bob shrugged.

"Did he go to the doctor?"

"No, Uncle Will hated doctors and hospitals. He'd been healthy all his life and prided himself on keeping fit and in shape."

"But you think he knew something was wrong?"

"Mentally, he was sharp as ever. When I saw him, he brightened up."

"What do you think it was?"

"I couldn't say. He didn't tell me, and I don't think he wanted to know. But he was acting worried about something. This guy used to bicycle miles a day and walk and run. You should've seen his muscles. His grip strength was way stronger than mine."

"Maybe he was trying to ask you for help?"

"Uncle Will was pragmatic and organized. I wasn't surprised he had it all planned out, even his own burial."

"He wanted to die?" I asked.

"Of course not. Uncle Will didn't have a death wish. But he was realistic and business-minded. He prepared for the future."

"He wanted to see you in person?"

"Yes, a phone call wouldn't do."

"Did he give you anything?"

"No. He just told me that if anything happened to him, to see his attorney."

CHAPTER TWELVE

Bob left to walk to the attorney's office, which was about two blocks down on Main Street, a short distance from the inn. He pointed to the direction on his way out.

I stayed behind to linger after breakfast. I settled down for another cup of black coffee while waiting for him to come back.

The front door slammed, pushed by a blast of wind, startling me. I heard footsteps, firm and clunky, come down the hallway straight to the dining room.

A man appeared, gray hair tousled by the wind, wearing a black coat. He stopped when he saw me sitting at the dining table with my coffee. "Fresh pot?" he asked.

"Yeah," I said, tilting my head toward the counter.

He rubbed his hands together like he was warming them up or anticipating the coffee, grabbed a mug, and poured himself a cup. "May I join you?" He gestured to the seat next to me.

I nodded.

"Jack," he said, showing an easy smile.

"I'm Eve," I said.

"So what brings you out to this neck of the woods?"

"I'm visiting. Here on spring break."

"Do you go to Colorado State?"

"Midway College."

He frowned. "Around here?"

"Back east, in the South."

"That's a long way to travel."

"I'm here with my friend, Bob Harding."

"Bob? I know him. Any friend of Bob is a friend of mine." His eyes lit up.

"So why are you here?" I asked.

He pushed his chair back, the legs scraping the floor. "You wouldn't believe me if I told you."

"I like stories. Tell me."

He arched his back, stretching it against the chair, and then relaxed. "I knew Bob when he was a kid. Actually, I'd heard of him before that, being his uncle Will's friend from way back."

"When did you and Will meet?"

"The first day of school. I'd stumbled in late to Professor Gainer's class. Got lost," he said. "But that's not a good excuse. Small-town kid, new experience going away to college. I knew no one there. The professor was lecturing and writing on the blackboard when I slipped in. Lucky for me, he had his back turned toward the students. Everyone had their eyes on the teacher—that is, everyone except this skinny kid with stringy, long hair who turned to look at me."

"That kid was Will?"

Jack nodded. "He saw me. My eyes darted frantically around the room, looking for an empty seat. He raised his hand and waved, catching my attention, and pointed to the empty seat beside him with his bookbag and an article of clothing dropped on top."

"He saved you," I said.

"I slipped into that seat as he removed his stuff, before the professor turned around. Just in the nick of time. Will and I became friends from that day on. Having each other's back, like his having my back on the first day."

"Ever since college," I said with a smile, urging him to go on.

"I was friends with Will for so long."

"When did you meet Bob?"

He hesitated, like he was collecting his thoughts. "I remember the worst day in Will's life was when he got word of his brother's and sister-in-law's deaths." His voice caught. He coughed to clear his throat before he continued. "Will was overcome with grief. His older brother had died in the prime of his life. It left a mark on him. Then there was this child left behind, Bob. Will didn't have the strength or desire to take care of him. It was all he could do to live through each day. Those were the darkest hours." Jack let out a long sigh.

"You met Bob then?"

He sat up. "Oh yes, getting back to that. I didn't know that much about kids, and I didn't want to make mistakes. But somebody had to take care of Bob, so I stepped up and made the first move."

I frowned, trying to picture him as a younger man, making this move.

"It's not what you think. I literally made a move. Across the state, into Will's house. They lived in the town of Ravine then. It was just temporary, until the dust settled, I told him. Will was relieved, and although he didn't show it, he told me years later how much he appreciated my help." He sighed. "And now he's gone. It's too late."

CHAPTER THIRTEEN

If I'd had a cigarette, now would have been the time to light up. No kidding.

Bob said he needed my help because of something that didn't feel right. I gave him space out of respect as he grieved the passing of his uncle. But I still didn't have a clear picture of what was going on. Was there more? Something else around the recent loss? Jack showing up?

I walked out the door and down the sidewalk, in the direction where Bob took off. The small town retained much of its character. Where once horse-hitching posts stood, they'd been upgraded to parking meters. Farther down was a general store, which kept the flavor of the Old West, with stains and nicks on the weathered storefront. The bank building screamed money, after it was renovated and standing slick with shiny black-gray marble. It stuck out, seemingly out of place.

It didn't take long to find the lawyer's office. I waited outside, favoring the sunshine with one side of my face. When Bob finished with the lawyer, I'd ask him. He was going to answer all my questions if he wanted my help. It was time. I was a firm believer that two heads were better than one. Especially when we'd worked together to help solve cases. There was no doubt about it.

I shivered as a breeze whipped my hair, twirling the strands and covering my face. I crossed my arms and held on to my thin sweater. The weather was at a turning point, as winter melted away and bared the ground for rebirth. The plants and flowers would soon push their way from the earth, thrusting upward and breaking the surface until they were free in the open air, their face to the sun, soaking the warmth and the light. It was one of my favorite times of the year, when spring sprang forward at the clock, and the days became longer. I knew this as sure as I'd lived for the past twenty seasons of spring. I knew it as sure as the calendar turned the page, the days marching forward.

I watched the people passing by, some wearing winter's catalog of dark clothes and shoes or sturdy boots. *Soon*, I wanted to tell them. I imagined this town in the summer, the streets full of hyperactive children out of school, dragging harried parents to go places and do things. The stores would be cool inside and inviting, a burst of air-conditioned chill greeting customers as they opened the doors.

They'd go to the ice cream store, selling homemade

batches of rich ice cream, thick and sweet, with just the right mixture to entice the taste buds. The good stuff. Not with cheap corn syrup substituting for real cream. It would be authentic, like the narrow stairs in the inn that wouldn't pass modern inspection in this day and age. People came here for the authenticity and the bygone days of the Wild West.

"Hey, I'm done," Bob called out as he walked up to me. His face looked more relaxed, and there was some color on his cheeks.

"Everything okay?"

"It wasn't as bad as I thought."

I certainly didn't want to pry, but I was dying to know. Was this the reason he came back here?

"Oh, I met someone back at the inn, after you left," I said.

"Do I know this person?"

"He says he's a friend."

Bob raised his eyebrows. "I'm not expecting anyone."

"He's an old friend of Uncle Will."

"What's his name?"

"Jack. He's at the inn."

"I'd say he's practically part of the family," Bob said as a boyish grin spread across his face. "Well, what are we waiting for? Let's go see him." I got a glimpse of the old Bob in that moment, of him in happier times.

"Okay," I said, leading the way.

I slowed down for Bob to catch up with me. "You coming?" I asked.

"I want to show you something first," he said, stopping to point across the street.

I peered in that direction, not knowing what to look for. "There are no buildings out there. Just trees and grass and flowers."

He crossed the street at the stop sign and took a path toward the green area.

I hesitated, then followed him.

A brick walkway laid out a path that took us from the town's Main Street to a square patch of green surrounded by planted trees and trails inside the area. "What's this ... a park?" I asked.

A pair of inviting metal chairs were anchored into cement at the entrance. A metal plaque was erected at the entryway. I walked closer to read the engraved text. The plaque simply stated that the park was dedicated in honor of William Harding, the mayor. I gasped, turning to Bob. "Your uncle Will ... he was the mayor?"

He nodded and grinned widely. "Yup. Uncle Will was elected mayor and he served for a number of years." His voice swelled with pride.

"What an honor."

"He blossomed here after we left Ravine. Gradually came out of his shell. He fell in love with this town and couldn't stop talking about it. Made strangers feel at home when they visited. That's how he got the idea of having a more modern inn. He purchased it. Then he remodeled the building, taking great care to preserve as much of it as he could. In its heyday in the nineteenth century, it was called the Golden Nugget

Saloon, and it had rooms upstairs for rent. They later changed the name to Prospect Inn. Will kept the name when he opened for business."

"Did people like it?"

"Well, word got around and more folks started coming. Pretty soon, Prospect Inn became a hit with tourists and travelers, so they had to turn away folks who had to go elsewhere."

"Where did they go?"

Bob turned around. "See that building down there past the end of the street? That's a new hotel, a modern one. It stirred up a lot of controversy, since it didn't fit in with the architecture of an authentic Old West town."

"Was there an old hotel originally?"

"Yes, there was a wooden house that had rooms to rent, which served as a hotel and a boarding house for weary travelers needing a place to stay. It wasn't fancy."

"What happened to it?"

"It decayed over the years because it hadn't been kept up. It finally got too expensive to upkeep. So they built a new one."

I squinted, narrowing my eyes to get a better look at the new three-story building, which was constructed of brick and mortar instead of wood. "I saw that earlier and wondered about it. It seemed out of place."

"The developers had deep pockets. There was a big fight, and some folks were upset. The townsfolk mostly. But the businesses sided with the developers, who promised the town would be booming, and as more people came and stayed longer and rented rooms, the more money they'd spend in the other establishments."

"What did your uncle do?"

"Well, he found himself caught in the middle. With different agendas. It made the news and there was a big splash. Uncle Will was politically savvy and led the way to brokering an agreement. In the end, they built the hotel at the outskirts of town."

"It's set apart," I said, "like an afterthought."

CHAPTER FOURTEEN

It was a brisk walk back to the inn, past the bank, the sheriff's office, and the hardware store.

"Your uncle ... did he die a natural death?" I asked.

"Will was found dead in his bed and purported to have died in his sleep."

"Did you talk often on the phone?"

"He did most of the calling. I'm afraid I wasn't good at keeping in contact, and I was lousy at returning his calls. I blamed it on classes and being busy," Bob said, his voice tinged with regret.

I kept silent and didn't interrupt.

"Sometimes it was a day or two before I got back to him. Who am I kidding? I was selfish and couldn't be bothered. Yeah, I was busy, but not too busy to spare a few minutes of my time." His fingers raked his hair.

"Maybe your uncle knew? A young man in college, first time away from home. Maybe he didn't expect you to be tethered to him."

"No," he sighed. "I let him down when he needed me."

"Did he ask you to do anything?"

He shook his head slowly. "No, he wasn't like that. You have to understand my uncle. He didn't want to be the weight on my shoulders. He gave me the freedom to fly away and make my way. He wanted me to live a full and satisfying life."

"That's what parents want."

"He was with me and supported me when my parents died. I withdrew into a shell, walking around in a daze. At night, I hugged my pillow and cried out for my mom. I screamed and cursed. Alternating between self-pity, rage, tears. And I blamed my uncle Will because he was there and it was convenient and there was no one else to take the blame."

I touched his sleeve lightly.

He wrenched his arm away from my fingers like he detested my pity. "Don't you see? I wasn't there for him," he said, his face twisted. "I thought I had my whole life ahead of me, and all the time in the world." Tears glinted on his cheeks. "I didn't know his time was up."

We'd arrived at the inn, standing in front and facing it. A hitching post, a remnant of the Old West, stood like a landmark of authenticity.

"Here we are," I said.

Bob leaned against the wood rail of the hitching post and appraised the building, looking it over from top to bottom. The post had been preserved.

I tapped the wood. It felt firm and hard, not soft and rotten, like someone had injected it with a strengthener.

"I'd like to visit Uncle Will's grave," he said, sounding sad.

"Is it far?"

"We can walk." He pointed to the edge of town, where a gentle hill and the steeple of a church rose to the sky at the highest point, overlooking the town. "He's buried in the church graveyard."

"Is there a flower shop nearby?" I glanced back, searching for it.

"Oh yes. It's that way, past the inn and farther down."

We walked toward the shop, the opposite way from where we came. No wonder I hadn't seen it.

"What was your uncle's favorite flower?"

"He was a rose guy. Will used to say that he preferred a flower with a strong, sturdy stem over a soft, fragile, wimpy stem any day. He said the thorns added character to the rose's woodier stems. A man's flower."

"I love the scent."

"Yeah, that too. But Uncle Will was more of a visual guy than olfactory."

"Any favorite color?"

"Naw, I think he'd be happy with any color we get except black."

"Ugh, I've never seen one of those. I don't think

you'd have to worry about that," I said, as I opened the door of the quaint little flower shop and went in.

The cozy shop was narrow and cramped. Ahead, an old-fashioned cash register sat on top of the counter. A basket of flowers was on a round table, and cut flowers in vases lined the shelves of a floral display cooler. An assortment of gift items—including chocolates and handmade items by local artisans—and cards, ribbons, and accessories catered to customers shopping for birthdays, anniversaries, and other occasions.

"May I help you?" A woman stepped out from the back, hearing the bell chime as the front door opened.

"Hi, we're looking for roses," I said.

She glanced at the cooler. "We have red roses, and carnations and sunflowers."

"Any chance you have any other colors of roses?"

"Let me check in the back," she said, disappearing behind the curtain to the rear of the store.

"What if that's the only color?" Bob whispered.

"We'll just have to see." I was optimistic.

The woman reappeared, a bunch of single-stem roses in each hand. "You're in luck."

I glanced at the long-stemmed pinks in one hand and whites in the other, and winked at Bob.

"We'll take them," he said.

She frowned, looking from left hand to right, and glancing across to the refrigerator. "Which ones?"

"The roses you're holding, ma'am," he said.

She nodded and put the roses on the counter. She

twirled a generous length of ribbon from the spool, cut it, tied it around the roses, and wrapped their stems in layers of white and pink tissue papers.

"How's this?"

Bob smiled his thanks. "It's perfect."

CHAPTER FIFTEEN

The new headstone, with its polished surface, stood out amongst the dusty, weather-worn stones in the graveyard.

"That's Uncle Will," Bob said.

I helped him place the roses on the grave. Glints of water drops hung on the petals, sparkling in the sunlight.

I walked away to give Bob some alone time. I made my way to the other side of the graveyard at the edge of the hill, overlooking the town nestled in the valley beneath the looming mountains.

It was peaceful up here. Undisturbed, the bees went about their business, and the wildflowers swayed in the gentle breeze. The humming of insects and chirping of birds blended in, providing a natural symphony for the beautiful land. I inhaled deeply, opening my lungs to the fresh air. There was something raw here, still, like it was wild and uncivilized.

I wondered how many lay buried, unadorned and nameless, here? Or left dead on the ground to rot or to be picked apart and eaten by scavengers?

I imagined the old Wild West, the pioneers who braved the way and faced the dangers of man and beasts and nature. Who were the strong ones who survived? Who became sick and injured? Who were the lucky ones? Who refused to be tied down and considered their saddles their homes? Who worked the mines? Fields? Had babies? Endured surgeries without modern medicine? Who were the men, women, and children who came before to this land?

I was the stranger here, a visitor to this place. A temporary stay for a few days. Yet I felt welcome. The birds and bees were my friends. The sun inviting. Even the wind caressed my face and whipped and tussled my hair. There was a pureness mixed in with energy, held in place as if there were a restlessness underneath, the memories of the Wild West stirring and calling.

Echoes of a past forged with human grit, determination, hard work or hard luck, blood, sweat, tears, and cries of joy, success, and the agony of failure. The survivors who lived or cheated to live. The gullible who gambled and lost. The immature who matured. The timid who became brave. The young who became old. The young who died young. The useful who became useless. The fertile who became barren and worn. Everyone had a story to tell. Some pretty, some not so pretty.

Who believed in God? In fate? Who carried them

when they could no longer walk? What gave them hope when life seemed hopeless? Who fought for their lives? Who gave up? Who had faith? Who believed in destiny? How many lives came through or lived here? This land that gave no one an easy time. It was hard-won, hard-fought survival. Humans did it. Animals did it. Every living thing. Until they died.

I felt grateful. I *was* grateful. For so many things. Even in my short twenty years that I walked this Earth, I'd seen so many things. Death was the worst. Its finality. Its coldness. I feared it, yet I wanted to understand it. For the living and for the dead. The inflicted violence and murder that stifled life. In the end, making sense. Finding justice for an unjust death. There was no going back, but maybe that was something to add to death, to allow them to rest in peace as the body turned to dust, back to earth.

"It's beautiful, isn't it?" Bob had snuck up behind me.

"Yes. I've never been out west before. Only seen it in movies and TV shows. You can't compare a TV screen to the real deal. It's indescribable."

"I fell in love the first time I saw it."

"I can see why. This quaint old Western mining town nestled in the foothills of these mountains."

"I'm glad you could come here on such short notice."

"Thank my mom. When I talked to her about your invite, she asked me if I wanted to go."

"I hoped you would after I worked up the guts to ask you."

"Mom urged me to go. Besides, she thought it'd be a good change of scenery, and I'd never been to Colorado."

"Well, I'm glad you came."

"Me too."

CHAPTER SIXTEEN

Bob kept his voice even and slow. "Uncle Will had been feeling unwell. He was a stubborn man, and he hated needles and hospitals. I tried to take him to the doctors when I came back during winter break, but he wouldn't have anything to do with them."

"I can understand that. My mom is the same way, but thank God she's healthy."

He squeezed his eyes shut. I waited for him to continue.

He shifted, glancing at something in the distance. "I wish I'd tried harder. Uncle Will had gotten crankier, and it became increasingly difficult to be around him. There were times I was so frustrated, I wanted to leave. But I felt ashamed even thinking those thoughts."

"Was he in pain?"

"I don't know. He didn't want to talk about his health. Every time I brought it up, he'd wave me off. He was stubborn, too. It seemed the older he got, the more he was that way."

"He dug in?"

"Yeah, he told me in no uncertain terms. I avoided conflict after that and chalked up his not feeling well to being under the weather, and maybe he'd get over it soon. Then I had to return to school when classes started."

"Any regrets?"

"In hindsight, I might have been firmer and insisted on him getting checked out. But it would have upset him." Bob straightened up and fixed his gaze on me. "I will *not* second-guess what shoulda, woulda, coulda been done."

"Please don't take that as being judgmental. You did what you could, and you came when he wanted you to. That's how you helped him."

"Sure."

"You didn't force him to do things against his will."

"Uncle Will was a proud man. He'd never have gone into assisted care or a nursing home. He had a strong will."

I thought about the pioneers, settlers, miners, and cowboys who forged their way west against all odds and the strong will they needed for survival. "Your uncle's will was what kept him going like the people who came before him."

"I admire him, not just because he raised me."

"He knows," I said.

"Uncle Will, I miss you," he cried out. "Why did you leave me all alone?"

I could hear the anguish, and I knew he was suffering. He had experienced tragedy and pain. First his parents. Now his uncle who had adopted and raised him. I couldn't imagine what Bob had gone through. In school, he'd kept his emotions in check. I, along with our friends, knew him as strong, steady, and reliable. He'd seen my fears, exposed on Snake Mountain and along Route 82, and calmed and soothed me. He was there for me, more than once.

I'd seen his pain and deep sorrow over the loss of a loved one. It saddened me to see my friend in such a state.

CHAPTER SEVENTEEN

We went our separate ways back at the inn. Bob to his room, and I to explore the town. There was plenty of daylight left, and it would be a pity not to enjoy it.

I thought about the events since my arrival and learning more about Bob's family. He had unfinished business. For one, the visit to the only lawyer in town, James Garrett. Maybe some other things were left unsettled, things Bob had not shared yet. Maybe he didn't have all the pieces and could not verbalize the specifics yet. Maybe he needed me to help figure it out. Grief had gripped him, and he was not able to move beyond that now. Maybe it was so raw and hurting that he was still in shock. I still wanted to give him space. I could use some myself.

Absorbed in my thoughts, I found myself at the park. My body had moved as if on autopilot. Entering the park, I felt the weariness spread over me. Each step took more effort than the last. My eyes lit on the benches under a tree, and I made my way there and sat.

The tragedy that Bob had encountered was more than any of my friends had. Even though I knew he had strength, he also had pride. It must have been difficult for him to ask me for help. He was having a hard time. It wasn't easy for him.

I didn't have to stop for hot chocolate that day at school, although it had become a habit. I could've gone there a few minutes before, or after. I didn't have an appointment. I wasn't expecting to see him. I mean, I certainly would have met with Bob, but he hadn't contacted me. If I had missed him that day, would he have tried to reach me later?

Bob was acting strange that day. Out of character. I think he hadn't made the decision to go back to Colorado until he met me. The thought had occurred to him. He'd blurted out the invite on the spot, along with the offer to pay for my airline ticket. It happened so quick. Just like that, I went from expecting a relaxing break at home to packing and dashing to the airport. Who knew I'd run into Bob that day? But sometimes it could be fate or destiny.

CHAPTER EIGHTEEN

I GOT UP FROM THE BENCH AND MADE MY WAY ACROSS the park to Main Street. I took a leisurely walk down the street, strolling aimlessly without a specific destination as I took in the sights. Passing by the general store, I stopped to stare in the window. The case in the front displayed an assortment of old-timey items. It was like stepping back into another era. I couldn't resist going in. Inside, it looked like an antique store, with worn-looking kitchen utensils, stacks of used plates, mugs and cups—some showing chips—cheap costume jewelry, old rusty tools, radios, and collectible items. I saw a few western hats and boots, and a bridle and saddle. There was a separate section with new hardware, pocket tools, local handmade items, jars of hard candy, and sodas for sale.

I missed antique shopping with my mom. It was one of our favorite pastimes when we got together. I strolled up and down the aisles, intent on finding a souvenir for her. I wanted something unique and Western, something she didn't already have. It helped that I had a good idea of what was inside her house already.

It was a case of "I don't know what I'm looking for, but I'll know it when I see it."

I finally chose a signed Waterford bowl and gave it to the clerk to ring up. She took off the tag that was tied with a string and identified the seller. Reaching under the counter, she pulled out a book, its cover frayed and well-worn, and searched for the item, confirming the price.

"Twenty-three dollars," she said.

I dug in my shoulder bag for cash, pleased it was very reasonable, and paid.

She whipped out a couple of sheets from a stack of old newspapers and wrapped my purchase, her fingers deftly working before adding the last touch, snagging a piece of clear tape from the dispenser.

"Thank you." I inspected the neat package and took it.

I hoped my mom would like my gift. Seeing the clerk wrap it in newspaper brought back childhood memories of me, tagging along with her, going to antique stores and flea markets. I had a feeling for what she liked and didn't like. It'd be hard to put it in words if someone asked me to describe it. On an instinctual level, I knew it the moment my eyes set on it. Price wouldn't have mattered to my mom. But she'd know if I'd spent time and put some thought on my selection. Here, it'd be more than the thought that mattered. A gush of gratitude and love filled my heart for my mother.

My feelings were lighter as I hurried back to Prospect Inn with my purchase. It'd been quite a day. The thought of a home-cooked meal and a quiet evening occupied my mind, eclipsing the gloom earlier. I reminded myself to stop by the small library area in the sitting room and check out the bookcase for some after-dinner reading. I traveled light, so I'd usually bring a slim paperback. But I had forgotten to bring any books this time.

I arrived at the inn and ran up the stairs to my room to unload my package. Then I went in the bathroom and washed up before dinner.

CHAPTER NINETEEN

The knock on the door was timed perfectly.

"Oh hey," I said, opening the door to see Bob standing there, looking well-rested.

"I heard you come in," he said.

"You napped?"

"Took a quick one. Where did you go?"

"Walked around and did some shopping. Found something for my mom."

"Good. You hungry?"

"I could eat a ton."

"We can get dinner now downstairs. They were doing a head count and asked me how many. I added our names."

"Okay, let's go," I said, closing the door behind me.

Some other guests were already seated in the dining room when we arrived. I glanced around but didn't recognize anyone. We picked one of the small square tables and sat.

The server was a matronly, middle-aged woman who brought over two filled plates and two settings rolled inside cloth napkins. I was eye-goggling our food. Bob's meal was identical to mine, except he had meat. We both had the same veggies.

"Apparently, everyone has the same menu for tonight. I told them to make yours no meat."

"Thanks for that." I glanced at the woman heading toward the kitchen. I had a strong suspicion she doubled as the cook.

She came back with a pitcher, filled our glasses with ice water, and left the pitcher on our table. "Dessert and coffee will be on the counter. Self-serve."

I smiled my thanks.

"Thank you. The food is delicious," Bob said.

Her face lit up.

"Do you know her?" I asked him after she left.

"Not well. She hasn't been working here long."

I thought back to Scarlett Bell that morning. The ugly scene had left an impression on my mind. "What about the housekeeper?"

"She's been here longer, some months back. Before the holidays."

"How did that come about?"

He shrugged. "Dunno. I was away at school."

I thought about the timeline. "Was he sick then?"

"Yeah ... no, she was here before that, I think."

I looked around and leaned in. "Does she live here?"

"No, she rents a place down the street."

"The girl—"

"That's her daughter, Serena."

"Does she also work here?"

"I think she helps occasionally."

"You said Will was stubborn about seeing doctors. Did he have a visiting nurse or health aide?" I asked.

"I doubt it. He wasn't an invalid. A few months ago, he was strong, athletic, and healthy."

"I get it. He wasn't an old man. But you said he got ill."

"Over the winter. He wasn't a believer in pills either."

"I guess he didn't get a flu shot."

Bob snorted, laughing. "Are you kidding?"

"Just checking. Men are like that sometimes. Tough guys don't go running to the doctor every time they have a sniffle, or aches or pains."

"He was like that."

"Think about all those cowboys and gunslingers. All the people out west back then. How did they manage?"

"I don't think about it. I like living in the twenty-first century."

"He reminds me of the Old West. He'd fit right in."

"He *was* a tough old bird."

"He wasn't an *old* man," I said.

"But even he needed help," Bob reminded me.

CHAPTER TWENTY

Jack showed up the next morning. I waved him over to the dining room, where Bob and I were seated. We had made plans to meet Jack for breakfast, after the long, exhausting day yesterday, which was an emotional one for Bob. Better to start fresh. He gestured to the coffeepot and made his way there, carefully navigating around the ladder where a man perched, switching out bulbs in the light fixture.

"Who's the guy on the ladder?" I whispered to Bob. "He got here after we arrived."

"Oh, that's Tommy, our maintenance guy."

I glanced at the guy, his long arms stretched over his head. His long legs and lean frame.

"Hi, Bob." Jack appeared and joined us, holding a brimming mug of coffee. He nodded in my direction. "Eve."

Bob studied him like it had been a long time since

they met and got up to greet him. "Jack, how long has it been?"

"It's been awhile." Jack gave him a warm hug before settling into the chair and taking a gulp of coffee. He rested his arms on the table, the mug between his hands.

"When was the last time we saw each other?" Bob asked.

"Umm ... reckon you were about twelve or thirteen. Thin as a stick, but almost as tall as you are now."

"Man, it's good to see you." Bob was grinning. "Eve says you guys already met."

"We met yesterday. Had a nice talk."

"She said you were looking for me."

Jack was silent for a moment. His eyes met Bob's and when he spoke, his voice was gentle. "I'm very sorry for your loss."

"You must miss him, too."

"We both do," Jack whispered.

"You saw him before he passed?"

"I ... I was too late."

"I don't understand," Bob sputtered. "Did you know that when you arrived?"

Jack shook his head. "I didn't know," he said. "I didn't know your uncle Will had died."

"Then why did you come?" Bob asked.

"Your uncle asked me to. Will had called me. We've kept in touch occasionally over the years, even though we hadn't visited each other." He stared down at his hand clutching the coffee mug. "I was surprised, and frankly pleased, to hear from him," he said.

"You had time to catch up?"

"Naw, not that kind of a call."

"What ... what kind of call?" Bob asked.

"A call for help."

"That's not like him. Uncle Will was like a cowboy on the range in the Old West, fighting the rustlers taking his cattle. He could've been a lawman breaking a fight over mining rights or between cheating card players. Or a gunslinger, the fastest gun, facing off the man who challenged him. Or ..."

I glanced at Bob. Saw his intense stare.

"Sounds like he was really tough," I said.

Bob swallowed. "Uncle Will?" he croaked.

Jack nodded.

"That's bull," Bob said emphatically, shaking his index finger to make a point. "I've never known Uncle Will to ask for help. From anyone."

"I agree. But that's what gave it away. Why I knew something was wrong," Jack said. He rubbed his chin. "Heck, I couldn't believe my ears. I asked him again."

"He was serious?" Bob pressed.

"Damn right he was. That man doesn't waste his breath. No joke."

"Did you know if he was sick at the time?" I asked.

"I could tell he was. I heard him. He was heaving and coughing."

"You think he wanted to see you because he was ill?"

He pondered my question, or maybe he was trying to remember.

"Initially, I jumped to that conclusion. But the more we talked, the less it made sense. If he was ill and still refused to see the doctor, then why was he calling me? I'm not a damn doc."

"Maybe he was sick," I said. "And maybe it was something else—something much worse."

"Did he tell you?" Bob asked.

Jack sighed, long and deep. If it were any longer, I think his lungs would be empty. "Will said he'd tell me in person. Said it was important. I could hear the urgency in his voice."

"You didn't know why?" Bob asked.

"No, but he sounded scared as shit."

"You came for your friend," I said.

"I gave him my word and said I would come when I could. But I didn't know I'd be too late."

CHAPTER TWENTY-ONE

After breakfast, I changed into my favorite faded blue jeans and a long-sleeved top, and I slipped out the door to Main Street. I needed to clear my head. I remembered passing by the sheriff's office the other day. I'd had an urge to walk in and talk to someone. But I wasn't an impulsive person. They'd question me and find out I had nothing to back up my suspicions. I had no evidence and nothing to show them. They'd laugh me out of the place. A lunatic with not a shred of evidence. But that was yesterday.

I saw the words "Prospector County Sheriff's Office," the lettering boldly etched on the glass pane of the front door and on a prominent sign on the building. Now I had a decision to make. Walk in and make a fool of myself. Maybe. Or turn around and walk away. I closed my eyes to stall for time. I knew what I had to do today.

I took a deep breath and turned the doorknob. But

it was moving, and the door swung open as I took a step forward, running straight into someone who was very tall. He was wearing a uniform. And he had a crooked grin.

"Whoa, what's the big hurry?"

My throat tightened. I was working my jaw but couldn't make a sound.

"Slow down," he said. "What's the problem?"

I stared at his name badge. Deputy Dillon.

My hands were working, twisting the bottom of my top. "It's about Will Harding," I blurted.

"Hold on. Tell me what happened. Start from the beginning, okay?" His sky-blue eyes were kind. Patient. Waiting.

I nodded. "I'm a journalism major at Midway College. Bob Harding is a classmate and friend. His uncle Will died. I ran into him right before spring break and Bob asked me for help, to come home with him. So I did."

"Is Bob in trouble?"

"No, not him." I glanced down at my shoes. They were covered in a layer of dust.

"Who, then?"

I moved my gaze up and looked him straight in the eye. I decided to tell him. "His uncle Will."

"You're not making sense. He's dead and buried."

I licked my lips. "I think Will Harding was in trouble toward the end. He asked his good friend Jack Holt for help before he died."

"Asking for help could be for different reasons.

Help with what? Maybe he needed money. A lot of it. That'd be a hard ask."

"No, I believe he was in danger. Men like him don't scare easy. From what I've heard, Will was tough and brave. It doesn't make any sense. But something or someone frightened him to the extent that he called Jack, his close friend, for help."

It was hard to read the deputy's face. It didn't show disbelief. "What proof do you have?"

"Bob and I just met and talked to Jack Holt. Will had called him for help."

"Did he say what kind of help?"

"No," I said. "Will died before he got here."

"Why are you here?"

"I think something terrible had happened to Will. Because he had an inkling, or it was more than just a suspicion, he reached out to someone he trusted for help. Maybe he didn't know the who, what, and why. Maybe he was trying to put the pieces together. Maybe he wanted to talk it out with a friend to prevent something."

"Will didn't tell Jack before he died?"

"No," I said. "Maybe someone found out about it and took action."

"Are you suggesting someone murdered him?"

"I don't think he killed himself or died of natural causes."

"If it's a homicide, who did it? What's the motive? How?"

I realized I sounded ridiculous, without a shred of

hard evidence. I said the only thing I could think of. "I don't know—yet. But I'm going to do what I can to find some answers. My friend Bob asked for my help. I can't let him down."

I meant what I said. My voice was serious and firm, but I was shaking inside. I didn't have a clue what happened to Will.

CHAPTER TWENTY-TWO

I LEFT MY CONTACT INFORMATION WITH DEPUTY DILLON and told him I was staying at Prospect Inn with Bob, and Jack Holt was also a guest there when we met him. The deputy had listened and made notes. He didn't promise he'd look into it, but he didn't say he wouldn't either. He gave me his number. I took that as keeping the door open. An encouraging sign.

I made my way back to the inn and leaned against the porch post. I recognized a couple of people from the dining room on the porch. They were talking in earnest about something. I opened the front door and went down the hall, passing the dining room. It was quiet. The tables had been cleaned off. I detected the faint lemon scent of furniture polish. I headed to the kitchen and peered in the doorway, hoping to see the chef. The slam of the refrigerator door alerted me to her presence.

"Hello?" I called out.

"Do you need something to eat?" the woman said, appearing from the back. She introduced herself as Luna.

"Oh no, I ate already. The food was delicious." I smiled.

"I keep a pot of coffee and hot water and tea bags on the counter all day. In the afternoon, there'll be a plate of homemade cookies."

"Yum, what cookies are you making today?"

"You like oatmeal raisin or chocolate chip?"

"Chocolate chip," I said with a grin.

"Be sure to stop by this afternoon." She winked.

I could see us getting along just fine. "I sure could get used to this," I said. I meant it. "So, how long have you worked here?"

"A few months."

"Will Harding hire you?"

She stopped what she was doing at the sound of his name. "Yes." Luna's voice dropped to a whisper. Her lips trembled. "Bless his soul."

"I'm so sorry. Can you please tell me what happened?"

"That day—" Her voice cracked, and she paused for a moment to pull herself together. "Will was an early riser. He'd beat me to it." She relaxed, erasing a frown. "We used to have a thing in the mornings. Like a habit where he stopped by the kitchen and said hello. Sort of like a running script. What time I got up depended on the menu, what I had to make. If I didn't need to be up so early, I stayed in bed and snuck in a few more minutes of sleep. That day, I'd overslept, and by the time I got to the kitchen and saw what time it was, eight o'clock, I kicked myself for being late." She sighed and placed the kitchen towel back on the rack.

I didn't say a word.

"I started working right away. Brewed a fresh pot of coffee and hustled to get breakfast ready. It wasn't until about thirty minutes later that it occurred to me I hadn't seen Will yet. I figured he had stopped by earlier, and because I was late, I thought he probably came and left. I figured he knew I was late, and he'd pop in and say good morning later, like he did every morning. We'd had this thing, you see. It sounds silly. I don't remember how it started. Somehow it became a habit—him stopping by in the morning. I'd brew a fresh pot of coffee and have it ready. He'd drink the first cup. He always said it was the best coffee he ever had."

"Wow, it must have been special."

"He'd start the day with it. Each morning. It's a powerful brew. Concentrated blend of dark roast with a bit of hazelnut grinds added, just enough to temper the bitter taste with the right flavor and mixture. It took some experimentation until I got it just right."

"Custom blended," I said. "For his morning coffee fix."

"Right. Every morning, we had this ritual. He got his first cup of his favorite coffee, and I got a 'good morning' and a smile. I'm happy and he's happy."

I steered the conversation back to that day. "On that morning you got up late, when did you see him?"

She sighed again. "After I made the coffee, he still hadn't shown up. I thought I'd missed him earlier, as he was usually a punctual guy. I couldn't get this thought out of my head that something was wrong. About another twenty minutes later, I took my apron off and took a quick peek in the dining room. It was quiet, except for the last couple lost in conversation, lingering over a late breakfast. I slipped out into the hallway and knocked on Will's office door. When he didn't answer, I tried his room. I pressed my ear to his door. The only sound was the ticking of the living room clock. Should I disturb him? I debated what to do, pausing at his door, halfway turning to leave. I finally jiggled the doorknob, and to my surprise it was unlocked."

I leaned in closer.

"When I opened his bedroom door, he was lying on his back, face up in the bed. In his underwear. His robe was open and rumpled. I called out his name, but Will didn't move."

I sucked in my breath, hoping against hope that her story would have a happy ending. But knowing how it would end.

Luna continued. "I couldn't tell if he was sleeping, so I walked up to the bed and tapped his arm lightly. That's when I noticed his chest wasn't moving, and where I could see skin, it had turned a pale color. I panicked. I didn't want to touch him."

"Then what did you do?"

"I was shaking. I backed away from the bed, one step at a time, until I reached the bathroom door. Then I turned around and ran straight into the bathroom. My heart was pounding, and I threw up. I slapped my cheeks and threw cold water on my face."

"Did you call nine-one-one?" I asked.

"Yes," she said, her voice dropping. "The sheriff and his deputy came with the ambulance. They rushed in ... didn't know ... thought he might still be alive."

"I'm so sorry."

Luna turned to me. "You know what I kept thinking the whole time?" Her voice quavered.

"What?"

"I never got to say good morning to him."

CHAPTER TWENTY-THREE

I went upstairs to see Bob. I knocked on his door and heard him say, "Come in."

"Am I disturbing you?" I asked, finding him sitting in front of his table.

"No," he said. "I looked for you earlier. Where'd you go?"

"I went for some fresh air. And I talked to Deputy Dillon." I watched for his reaction, realizing that maybe I jumped the gun before talking this over with Bob. "Maybe I should've discussed it with you first."

He wasn't upset. "You did what you had to do. I know how you are. You told him about Uncle Will?"

"Yes. After what Jack told us, I had to. The deputy may look into this. I'll still help. But I think they needed to be brought in on what's going on."

"To investigate?" Bob said.

"Yeah, and I just talked to Luna. Found out she was the

one who discovered Uncle Will. It looked like he'd died in this sleep. He was still in his underwear. Had a robe on. Was his death due to natural causes or something more sinister? Maybe it was meant to look like he had died in bed. Maybe that's why the sheriff didn't look into it."

"That's why I need your help."

"Do you know of anyone who'd want to kill your uncle?"

"Not off the top of my head, but you know I've been away in school. Although I've come back home on breaks, holidays, and summers and worked at the inn. Uncle Will has taught me a lot about running the inn, and I've tried to stay on top of things here as much as I could."

"We could ask around, find out if he's been having trouble with anyone. You mentioned the honorary dedication at the park. Maybe someone was jealous. What about the fight over the building of the new hotel? Did he make enemies?" I rattled on while my brain was in overdrive.

"So we need to look at suspects and the motives." I picked up on an undercurrent of energy in Bob's voice as he sat up in his chair.

"We should make a list of who was here the day he died," I said, taking a sheet of paper from his desk and writing "Luna."

"I can check our reservations for that day," Bob said, opening a laptop. "Let's see if my old password still works."

I stood next to him and peered at the screen as he typed.

"Hot diggity, I'm in. I'll check the date for the night before. The system will show pre-payments and the booking information at the time reservations were made. Sometimes people cancel, or don't show up, which is really rare. When that happens, Uncle Will updates the system and puts a note in there to explain."

"Your uncle may have died that night or in the wee hours of the morning. Did they do an autopsy?" I asked.

"Nope, they didn't."

"That's right. They wouldn't have if they thought he died in his sleep."

The calendar popped up on the screen. He clicked the date and four names appeared.

I jotted them down. Mr. and Mrs. Baldwin. Mr. Johnson. And Mrs. Fields.

"How long did they stay?"

"The Baldwins left that day." He clicked on more dates. "Looks like Mr. Johnson stayed one more night, and Mrs. Fields, also."

"Do you have their phone numbers?"

"They should be there. We get their addresses also, along with their credit card and the billing information." He went back to the registration tab and typed in their names. "I'll print out the information for all the guests."

"What about the staff?" I asked. "Do we know who was working other than Luna?"

"Mrs. Bell works every day, but she's usually only here for half a day at the most. Between the time guests check out and the new guests check in. Occasionally, Serena helps if she's busy with a lot of rooms to clean."

"Do they often have a shouting match in the hallway?"

"I think you caught them on a bad day. Serena is usually well-behaved."

"Who else works here?"

"Mr. Roth."

"I don't think I've met him."

"He's the bookkeeper slash accountant. Mr. Roth isn't here every day. He comes about once a quarter. Uncle Will set aside some space in his office and he works there."

"Does he have a set time?"

"No," Bob said. "Uncle Will wasn't that strict about his schedule. He let him come and go when it suited him, as long as the work got done and there were no problems."

"He must have been very trusting."

"Will said he was very lucky. And he had to get on Roth's good side. Something about him being irreplaceable."

I chuckled. "Hey, no one's irreplaceable."

"He is. At least to Uncle Will, he proved his value and trustworthiness."

"Okay, I get it."

"Oh, and there's the maintenance guy, Tommy."

"Right, I saw him on the ladder yesterday changing light bulbs while we had breakfast with Jack."

"Actually, he's quite handy, and he can fix practically anything."

"Good to know," I said with a wink. "Does he have a set schedule, or is he on call?"

Bob clicked a few more times. "He's on call. Technically twenty-four seven, but he keeps it to emergencies only in the evenings and on weekends."

"What does he do?" I asked.

"We have a running list of things, such as maybe fixing a leaky toilet, installing new tiles, repairing wall plaster, changing a light switch, replacing window trims, painting, whatever work needs to be done. He checks ahead and orders materials and gets tools and stuff. If it's a big-ticket item, he has to get approval before he orders."

"Sounds like there's flexibility."

"To an extent. It's figuring out what to prioritize, how much time, and the cost."

"What happens if he needs more time?"

"We make adjustments. He puts his time in the system, along with the cost of materials and other items."

"So he's not full-time here. Does he have other jobs?"

"He does. Word got out quick when he was looking for work. Other businesses keep him busy. He's good mechanically and also knows his way around electrical and plumbing."

"Sounds like he's skilled in many areas and in demand," I said, adding his name to the list.

Bob printed out the guest list with their contact information and handed me a copy. "Meanwhile, we can get started on these people."

CHAPTER TWENTY-FOUR

We worked the phones and made our way down the list of guests. I called the couple, Mr. and Mrs. Baldwin. The wife answered the phone. I introduced myself and explained the reason we were calling, about the death of Will Harding. She was shocked to hear about the unexpected tragedy.

"If you could help us out," I said.

"We'd just got back home from our trip."

"Why stay one night at Prospect Inn?"

"It was our second honeymoon. A celebration of our twenty-fifth anniversary. We planned this trip to retrace the steps of our first honeymoon."

"You stayed here twenty-five years ago?"

"Yes," she said. "My goodness, how fast the years had flown. Back then, John and I, well, when we met, we were both practically penniless. But we were young, happy, and in love."

I heard a man's voice, a hum and a rustling, and

what sounded like affectionate pecks on the cheek.

"Now, where was I?" She came back to the phone, sounding breathless.

"You were both young—"

"Yes, yes. And we decided to re-create the same route we took back then. When I called to make the reservation, I wasn't sure the place was still there and open. We lucked out."

"Why did you stay only one night?"

She laughed, deep and throaty. "You're thinking we have the money now to live it up? You're not wrong. We could have stayed longer, even a week or two. But the first time we'd stayed one night."

"I see," I said. But I wouldn't have stayed just one night. That was just me talking, so I kept it to myself. Time to change the subject. "Are you and your husband light sleepers?"

"My husband, no. Definitely not. I can be, sometimes, unless I'm really tired."

"In the evening and overnight during your stay, did you see Mr. Will Harding or hear any noise from his room?"

She paused like she was thinking hard—I hoped.

"Our room was upstairs. We could hear if someone was coming up or going down the stairs. But from where we stayed, we couldn't have heard anything from downstairs."

I waited for her to continue.

"We had dinner downstairs. I remember it was pot roast. I even remarked to John that it was delicious, perfectly cooked and flavorful. I moaned and said I'd never tire of eating this."

"Did you sit with the other guests?"

"We picked the small table. I wanted it to be cozy and romantic. Just the two of us. Frankly, I was too busy enjoying my dinner and conversation with John. I didn't pay attention to too much else."

"When was the last time you guys saw Mr. Harding?"

"He wasn't in the dining room when we had dinner." She paused like she was having a hard time recalling. "Well, I think it was in the late afternoon sometime. We'd gone out for a walk and came back to the inn for the afternoon refreshment, homemade cookies, which were in the dining room. He passed us on our way in and said hello."

"Did you speak to him?"

"Just briefly when he greeted us, and introduced himself, and asked how our stay was."

"Which way did he go?"

"Down the hall. I'm assuming he went to his office or room."

"How do you know that for sure?"

"Well, first, he didn't go outside because the front door didn't open and close."

"How could you tell?"

"I know because I would've heard the little bell ring."

"Did he go upstairs?"

"There's no way anyone could have crept up the rickety wood stairs without the creaking noise."

"Do you know where his office is?"

"It's on the other side of the house, apart from the dining room and the front parlor, because I saw his name on the door. I heard a door close shortly after he passed us, which could be his office."

"Okay, that makes sense. About what time did you see him?"

I heard a muffled sound like a hand had covered the phone's receiver, and her yelling something to John.

"The tea hour was from three in the afternoon until four-thirty. I remembered we had gone out into town and stopped in front of the mercantile store and debated whether or not to go in. John was pulling my arm and urging me to go in. He was eager to see the stuff. But I had made up my mind about teatime and I didn't want to miss it. I remember we both checked the time, and it was four-twenty. I said to John, 'We have ten minutes to get to the inn before teatime ends. No time to go shopping,' and he didn't argue and went along with me."

"So you made it to the tea and saw Will Harding?"

"We did," she said. "We *sure* did. Mr. Harding made an impression when I first met him. I liked him right away."

CHAPTER TWENTY-FIVE

Bob stood up after leaving a message for the other two guests. "Let's take a walk."

"A breath of fresh air to clear our heads?" I said.

We left the inn. It was gray outside, the clouds heavy and low. The temperature had risen a few degrees according to the meteorologist on TV, but the forecast was rain by late evening.

"Did you have a good meeting with the attorney?" I asked.

A flicker of irritation crossed his face. "He had me sign some papers. Couldn't do that over the phone."

"He's handling your uncle's affairs?"

"Yes," Bob said. "He handled Uncle Will's business for many years and now he's the executor, remember?"

I'd hit a sensitive spot. It was none of my business.

"Did your uncle have recent troubles with anyone?"

"I couldn't say since I've been away in college, although I've come home on holidays, breaks, and the summer. I know things were stirred up over the building of the new hotel a while back, but it's calmed down since then."

"Why did you ask me for my help?"

"You know why," he said tersely.

Bob could be stubborn. I counted to ten in my head.

"I feel like we've come to a dead end. I'm grasping at straws and coming up empty. Your uncle *may* have died suspiciously. We don't have any suspects. We don't have a motive. We don't have any proof." I waved in frustration.

"Do we have a bright side?" he asked.

"What we know. We know Uncle Will called his old friend Jack and asked for help before he died. The Prospector County Sheriff's Office is probably looking into his death now. Maybe it's murder. We made a list of the people who were at the inn that night. We have a list of the staff. We have the records of the guests, when they checked in, and when they checked out, as well as their address, phone, and contact information. We'll know more when we talk to them."

He nodded. "Mrs. Bell has already gone for the day. Tommy is on call. You've already talked to Luna."

"Anyone else?"

"I can go into the system and check who worked that day and the hours they were paid. Sometimes they work over the regular schedule when we're busy. Uncle Will was particular about keeping the time and paying them extra when they stayed. He never nickeled and dimed the staff. He believed in fairness and loyalty."

"Could someone have worked and not marked their time sheet?"

"Not unless they didn't want to be paid," he said. "Uncle Will had switched over to electronic time keeping. The staff signs in and signs out on the computer. It helped him with records and accounting, especially with the irregular work hours and schedules."

"Are you aware of any disagreements between your uncle and the employees?"

He ran his fingers through his hair. "I think there have been some in the past."

"Major ones?"

"I think for the most part, they weren't that bad. Although ... Scarlett Bell has a forceful personality," he said, pointing upstairs, "as you saw yourself."

I acknowledged that with a small smile. "They butted heads?"

"Yes, on a couple of occasions that I'm aware of. When she first started, she was insistent on not wearing a uniform, which had been the tradition before."

"She refused?"

"That was a sticky point of contention from the beginning. My uncle can be stubborn, but he'd been quite clear on this matter."

I frowned. "So how did she ..."

"It's a mystery to me. Uncle Will wouldn't talk about it afterward. Not even to me. He considered the matter closed."

"Sounds like he didn't like conflict."

"Who does? But I had a feeling there was something else."

"You said there were a couple of occasions," I said. "What was the second disagreement about?"

"I can't think of it at the moment. I could be wrong."

CHAPTER TWENTY-SIX

THE SHARP RINGING OF BOB'S CELL PHONE STARTLED ME, disturbing our conversation. He picked it up and checked the call display. "I don't recognize this number."

He answered and put it on speaker. "Hello?"

"Bob, I got you message. This is Mr. Johnson, calling you back."

"Yes, thanks. Hey, we're contacting guests who stayed at Prospect Inn recently. I see you stayed two nights. Did you enjoy your stay?"

The guy made a snorting sound. "Oh, it's one of those calls," he muttered. "If you're calling for my feedback for a chance to win a prize, I'm not interested."

"Actually, no," Bob said. "I'm asking for your help. My uncle passed away during the time you were here, and we're asking for any information regarding that time."

"You got to be kidding. I can barely remember what I ate for breakfast this morning."

"Do you recall seeing him the first night you were here?"

"Hey, I can't help you."

"Did you see him at all?"

"I don't recall."

Then the line went dead.

Bob and I exchanged looks.

"Well, that was weird," I said. "He wasn't even curious about it."

"Then why did he call back?"

I shrugged. "Maybe he was expecting something else."

"Do you think he really doesn't remember?"

"Your guess is just as good as mine. Now I'm curious why he was in town."

"Uncle Will would have handled the reservations then."

"Who else may have known?"

"Maybe Roth. The ever-efficient accountant, Mr. Roth," he mused.

CHAPTER TWENTY-SEVEN

Our list of potential witnesses and suspects had produced little information. The timeline was one of our unanswered questions.

Bob took me to his uncle's office again. "I'm not a fan of the narrow stairs and the flimsy railing and worried about him falling. I had urged Uncle Will to take the rooms downstairs for his safety. To my relief, he agreed without much of a fight."

I gestured toward the rest of the house. "What do you know about its history?"

"I know the inn had survived damages, both man-made and from nature. A part of a room had been burned at one point. Each time, the inn was rebuilt as it stood its ground and underwent restoration. It's seen better days, at the height of the gold-mining boomtown. It saw its worst days, when it almost became a ghost town after people abandoned it and left. The inn needs a coat of paint again, but who knows how many coats are under the present layer? The owners over the years had repaired and maintained the place. But it wasn't until the revival of the town as a tourist attraction that it underwent a major renovation. The windows were in terrible shape and had to be replaced, along with wood on the frame that had rotted. The upstairs rooms were upgraded."

"What about the floors?"

"There was a lot of wear and tear, especially on the authentic wood floors and the flimsy stairs."

"In pretty awful shape?"

"Yeah, the old wooden floors had dings, scratches, dents, marks, holes." Bob laughed. "But they sure had character!"

"That's irreplaceable," I said.

"When Uncle Will bought the place, he hired an interior decorator. They painted the walls," Bob said, waving around the room. "They modernized and expanded the kitchen, and added a laundry area with a commercial-grade washer and dryer. New furniture and curtains brought a fresh look, while maintaining the style with a contemporary feel. It was a lot of work, but the finished product was worth it. The decorator had connections to a travel writer and successfully got an article published in a travel magazine. Pictures accompanying the story showed off the adorable inn. An architectural magazine and a catalog about places to visit in Colorado featured it."

"I'm impressed."

"It was Uncle Will's last project," Bob said, "and his pride and joy."

We stood at the door of the office. It was closed. His name, William Harding, was on a brass plate tacked to the door. I stared—it was polished. Brazen. As if it dared anyone to take it down. As if it guarded a dead man's office and dared anyone to intrude.

"The next room is his private quarters, comprising a bedroom and bathroom," Bob said. "The doors for these rooms are usually closed, and they can be locked. Uncle Will liked the separation of space between his public and private areas."

My phone rang. I glanced at the unfamiliar number with a Colorado area code that interrupted our conversation. I answered briskly. "Hello?"

"Deputy Dillon here. Is this Eve Sawyer?"

"Yes," I said, gesturing to Bob and mouthing, *"Sheriff's office."*

"Are you with someone?"

"I'm with Bob Harding."

"I need the two of you to come down to the sheriff's office and bring the man that you spoke to about Uncle Will."

"What's this about?"

"I need to talk to Bob and get a statement from both of you."

My eyes met Bob's. "Sir, we'll be right there. But I don't know where Jack is."

I ended the call. "The deputy I mentioned wants to see us. Both of us."

"It's urgent?" he asked.

"I believe so. Do you know how to get ahold of Jack?"

"Yes, his contact details are in the inn registry."

"Get his number. We have to go now."

CHAPTER TWENTY-EIGHT

The RECEPTIONIST AT THE SHERIFF'S OFFICE WAS expecting us and ushered Bob and me into Deputy Dillon's office.

"Have a seat," he said.

The deputy pulled out a folder and opened it. I recognized the newspaper articles about my previous cases inside. The deputy had done his homework.

He tapped his finger on the paper. "You didn't tell me about the cases you helped to solve," he said, smiling.

I felt my face redden and looked down quickly in embarrassment. I was humble and preferred to keep my accomplishments to myself. But one thing I knew for sure now. He'd taken me seriously. And that's why he'd called me back.

He turned to Bob. "William Harding was your uncle?"

"Yes," Bob said. "And he raised me after my parents died."

"Where were you when he died?"

"I was away at Midway College," he said. "Eve and I are students."

"Were you surprised to hear about his death?"

Bob didn't reply.

"He's still grieving," I said, to fill in the silence.

"I'm sorry, this is hard for you. But Eve shared with me her concerns after this man, Jack, came to see you."

"Jack was Uncle Will's longtime close friend," Bob said. "At breakfast, Jack talked to us. He said Uncle Will had called him for help before he died."

"Did he say why?" Dillon raised his eyebrow.

Bob shook his head. "No, he said he was going to go see Uncle Will. But he died before they met in person. Will was going to tell him."

"Do you believe this man?"

"I know he's a good friend. He and Will were close, like two peas in a pod. I have no reason to doubt him."

"You think he's telling the truth?"

Bob shrugged. "I have no reason not to."

"Is he still here?"

"I'm not sure. I assumed he was planning on leaving after talking to us."

"Do you have his phone number?"

"Here's Jack's cell," Bob said, reaching in his pocket for the piece of paper he'd scribbled it on.

"Thanks. So you asked Eve to come to Colorado with you, right?"

"Yes, that's correct."

"Why?"

"I ... I thought she could help me."

"Because of her ability to solve cases?"

"Yes."

"Did you or do you still have suspicions?"

"I thought I had, in my mind. But in the light of day, it sounded unbelievable. I had no concrete evidence. Until Jack talked to us about Uncle Will."

"Bob, you're his next of kin, so I'm letting you know." The deputy cleared his throat. "I've discussed this with Sheriff Matt McCain. We're going to open an investigation into Will Harding's death."

I sucked in a breath. An investigation. A suspicious death?

Bob sat quietly, like he was thinking it over. "What do you mean?" he finally said, his voice shaky.

"We're going to work this case. Investigate how he died, whether he died of natural causes in his sleep or not."

"Do an autopsy?" I asked.

"If we have to, we'll exhume the body."

"Uncle Will was in his fifties when he died and had been in relatively good health before. When he started feeling sick, I urged him to see a doctor, but he refused. Could this be related?" Bob asked.

"Is it possible that he was poisoned?" I asked.

"We're looking for evidence," Dillon said.

"Of course." My eyes trailed across his desk, landing

on the newspaper clippings. "But if there's anything we can do ..."

His fingers tapped the papers. "Just let us do our thing."

"I'll do that," I said.

"And thank you for reaching out to us with your suspicions of foul play in Will's death. We will do a thorough investigation," he said.

CHAPTER TWENTY-NINE

WE WALKED OUT OF THE PROSPECTOR COUNTY Sheriff's Office into the warmth of a spring day. My mood lifted immediately.

Bob was quiet. He hadn't said a word since we left Deputy Dillon's office. I couldn't tell what he was thinking, but I was sure his sullen mood needed no translation. Maybe he was upset at me now for going to the authorities. I knew I was doing the right thing and trying to protect him as he grieved. This was one of those times it was better to take action—at least I felt that way. No disrespect. It was my call, and I took responsibility for it. Although I hadn't expected the deputy to have done his due diligence and looked into me before he acted so quickly. He was decisive and gave us the courtesy of this meeting.

I was determined to keep my spirits up. I no longer felt like a hamster spinning his wheels alone. The wheels of the law were also put in motion.

"Hey, let's go walk in the park," I said cheerfully.

I snuck a quick glance at Bob. He was a man of few words, but right now my count was zero. I stepped up my pace and walked ahead of him to the entrance of the park. I didn't wait for Bob before I went past the sign and inside. If he wanted to join me, he was welcome. I wasn't letting anyone spoil my mood.

I picked up the sound of footsteps behind me. I smiled to myself, not bothering to turn around.

The shrill sound of police sirens startled me. I turned my head toward the noise.

"Hear that?" I stopped and took a step back, bumping into Bob. "Where's it going?"

"It's getting louder," he said.

I could see the flashing blue lights and the cars approaching. "It's ... it's coming toward us," I said, gripping his sleeve.

By now, the cars had stopped, and men in uniforms rushed out. They ran toward the park.

"Get back!" one officer shouted in our direction.

I moved farther back, Bob along with me. My curiosity took over. I pulled him over to where a crowd had gathered.

"What happened?" I asked a middle-aged man with a dingy cowboy hat and clumps of unmanaged brown hair slipping out from under it.

"I think somebody discovered a body."

I gasped. "Are you sure it's a body?"

He shrugged and didn't answer.

Someone in uniform rolled out yellow tape, separating the expanding crowd of onlookers from the crime scene. By this time, the ambulance had arrived and joined the others. I recognized Deputy Dillon. A chill ran down my spine. Who could it be? I squinted and could barely make out a person lying prone on the grass. It was too far to see, or to even guess, if it was a man or woman.

I made my way closer, squeezing between the gaps in the onlookers with Bob tight behind me.

My body pushed against the yellow tape.

I blinked and rubbed my eyes, disbelieving what I could see. I locked eyes with Bob.

There was no mistaking the blue plaid shirt splattered with blood and the black boots with the shiny toe tips sticking out.

CHAPTER THIRTY

A skinny, tall young man wearing a sheriff's office uniform and the name tag "Bragg" walked toward the growing crowd of people.

"Folks, please stay back behind the tape," he said, directing us. I could imagine him as a cowboy with his handsome hat, sitting up in his saddle as if he were corralling cattle behind the fence. "Who discovered the body?"

An elderly couple in the front raised their hands.

"This way, please," he said, a pen in one hand as he flipped open a notepad. Bragg lifted the crime scene tape for the couple to pass through and eased them away from the crowd to a quieter spot. Out of earshot.

Deputy Dillon saw us and nodded before walking away to interview the elderly man and woman.

Bragg returned, moving among the crowd, taking down names and contact information and asking if anyone had witnessed the act or seen the perpetrator.

As soon as he had taken our information and talked to us, I yanked Bob's arm, pulling him away. He resisted, hesitant to leave the scene, his eyes fixed on the body as if they were glued to a horror movie.

"Do you recognize the shirt?" I asked, my voice shaky. "It ... it ... looks just like the one Jack was wearing."

His face blanched. "You think it's him?"

"How can this be? It can't be him." I wished I could unsee what I saw. I wished it weren't real.

"No, this is not happening," Bob muttered in disbelief.

I worried about him. Every member of his family had died. His parents, and Uncle Will, and now Jack.

I struggled to find the right words. But my mind was blank. All I could think of doing was to reach out and hug him. I needed that as much as him.

"Whoever did this may still be in town," I said, changing the subject.

Bob's eyes flew wide open, scanning the crowd nervously. "You think that person is here, watching?"

"Maybe. It's not unheard of for criminals to return to the scene and mix in with the onlookers. Or be close by in town."

"Morbid. I don't get it. Who would want to do this? Do you think it has anything to do with Uncle Will?"

"We need to go," I said. "This may take a while."

"Where to?"

"The inn. I want to see when he checked in and how long he was planning to stay."

"You're right. He never mentioned it specifically."

"I assumed he would leave after we talked. It didn't occur to me he'd stick around. Or why."

"Assuming his business was to talk to Uncle Will, which didn't happen, so he lost the opportunity to find out. Who knows what was scaring my uncle?"

"I wonder who else knew he was in town, and why."

"Was anyone else in the dining room when he talked to you?"

I thought about it. "No, I was the only person by the coffee station when he came that time."

"And when we both talked to him, it was just us."

"He may have talked to others at the inn."

Bob sighed. "He was my friend too. Uncle Will was all I had, and Jack was like family back then."

"But he left."

"He did. I was never told exactly why. Even though I was a child, I knew something drove him away."

"You think he would have stayed otherwise?"

"Maybe."

"Okay, let's get back to the inn," I said.

"I wonder if he'd checked out?" Bob said.

"It seems he would've taken his luggage in that case. Why would he go to the park if he was leaving?"

"Should we tell Deputy Dillon?" Bob asked.

I glanced back, sweeping across the crime scene. "They're busy now. Dillon knows about Jack from what we've told him. Why don't we see if we can get more information before we call him? I'm having a hard time holding my investigative curiosity in check."

"Sounds good."

"Let's go," I said. "It's one reason I love small towns with one main street. You can walk almost anywhere."

CHAPTER THIRTY-ONE

The laptop sat on Bob's table. I flipped the lid up and turned the screen around to face him.

"Can you check the registrations?" I scooted it toward him without waiting for a response.

He typed in his password and accessed the inn's guest information.

I stood beside him and leaned over his shoulder. The registration page popped up.

Bob pointed to the list. "We had four guests registered who stayed here last night. That includes you, me, Mrs. Barnes, and, of course, we know Jack was here."

"There you are," I said, reading the names. "Mr. Jack Holt."

"He was a guest when you and I met him."

I looked at his registration. "He stayed two nights, so he's supposed to check out today. When's the checkout time?"

"By eleven."

"Does your system show the exact time he checked out?"

He shook his head. "No, our system isn't that fancy."

I squinted and frowned. "How would the inn know when guests leave?"

Bob laughed. "The old-fashioned way. When the guests leave, they return the check-in envelope, which has their name on the outside, put the key back inside, and put it in the basket in the front room."

"Okay, the reverse of check-in. How clever."

"It's run in a more old-fashioned way than state-of-the-art technology."

I got it. "The best of both worlds." My cell phone rang. I pulled it out of my purse and answered on speakerphone, whispering to Bob, "It's Dillon."

"Eve?"

"Oh hi, Deputy Dillon. I have Bob with me on speaker."

"Where are you?"

"We're back at the inn."

I heard muffled speech and noises in the background. "Don't touch anything in Jack Holt's room," Deputy Dillon said. He sounded stressed, not the calm guy I spoke to earlier in his office. "Just stay there. We're on the way."

"But ... but he—"

"Save it. Tell me when I get there."

Then he ended the call.

I held the phone, my mouth parted open, and finished the sentence. "... may have already checked out."

"We need to see if his door was locked," Bob said.

"Why?"

"Well, the guests leave their doors unlocked when they check out. Remember, the key is in thc envelope downstairs. Mrs. Bell would know when she sees it, and that lets her know when she can come up and clean the room, change the sheets, replace the towels and toiletries."

"She would lock up after she cleans?"

"Yes, we don't allow anyone in a clean room until the next guest arrives. I think it's code—a hygiene thing."

"Well, let's go," I said.

THE POUNDING of the door left no doubt it was the sheriff's office, with someone shouting, "Open up!"

We rushed downstairs, Bob making it to the door first. I admit, his legs were longer, and I had to catch up. I was right behind.

"Ready?" he asked, turning the doorknob.

I took a breath and stood by his side.

Deputy Dillon was the first one in, followed by Bragg, looking fresh faced and eager and probably ten years younger than Dillon.

"How is he?" Bob asked. "I saw the ambulance. Is he badly injured?"

Dillan's face softened, pausing before answering. "He's dead."

124

CHAPTER THIRTY-TWO

I LAGGED AS THEY CLIMBED THE STAIRS. HEARING A sound on the first floor, I stepped down and caught sight of someone going around the hallway toward Will's office.

I placed my feet on the well-worn wooden floor, walking slowly and quietly, muscles tensed. As I slid my body along the wall, I saw the door to Uncle Will's office was slightly open. I paused. A faint squeak of the old chair reached me. I swung my leg to the other side of the door, which was open, and pushed it wider with the tip of my shoe.

A man was sitting in front of the desk, shuffling papers. His head was down as he concentrated on the task at hand. He didn't see me.

I coughed in the doorway.

He looked up, but his expression wasn't a guilty, caught-red-handed look. It was more of an irritation, like *go away*. Like I'd disturbed him. Like he didn't care who I was and couldn't be bothered.

"Excuse me," I said politely. "This is Uncle Will's office. Who are you?"

He glanced at me briefly. "Who are *you*?"

"I'm Eve Sawyer. Bob Harding invited me to stay here as a guest."

He straightened up, putting his hands on the edge of the desk and giving a little push, and studied me. He maintained his aloofness. Even the mention of Bob's name didn't change this man's expression. I knew then not to expect a warm welcome.

"If you're looking for Bob, I'm the wrong person to ask."

"I'm not. Who are you?"

"Roth. Will Harding's accountant."

"You share this office?" I asked, my eyes making a point, looking to the smaller desk across the room.

"Yes," he snapped. Then he went back to what he was doing, ignoring me.

I straightened and walked into the room. Stood right in front of him, facing the desk, my hips pressed against the edge of the hardwood.

"Are you aware one of our guests was just murdered?"

He looked up from the stack of papers in his hand.

I had his full attention. A flicker of surprise crossed his features. It was genuine. A person couldn't fake that look.

"Who?"

"The man was Jack Holt. He checked out this morning. We don't know the exact time. He was a friend of Uncle Will's."

Roth leaned back into the chair and it appeared to sink down, as if the weight of my words pressed him down, or he needed the seat to steady him.

"Were you here this morning?" I asked. Maybe he knew something. If Jack was a total stranger, would the accountant have acted this way? Maybe he saw him or talked to him?

"I was here."

"Do you have regular working hours?"

He shook his head. "I have flexible time. Will and I had this arrangement. As long as I got the work done, he didn't care when I came and went."

"How long have you been here today?"

"Since about ten this morning."

"Were you planning to work all day?"

Roth sighed. "This is my busy season."

I frowned, tilting my head.

"Tax time," he said. "Will Harding usually prepared his stuff and put all the things together that I needed and gave them to me before I did the taxes. But this year, he didn't have a chance."

I got it. It explained his frustration. "So you were looking through his papers for what you needed?"

"Yes." His voice squeaked as it broke with emotion.

I heard his pain. Death was a hard thing to process, and each person dealt with it in his or her own way.

"I'm sorry," I whispered. What else could I say?

I glanced around. The desk had been cleared. Instead of the messiness I saw the other day, it was organized. I saw neatly stacked papers in two piles. Pens lined up so straight, it suggested obsessive-compulsive behavior. Paper clips confined inside a magnetic container.

My eyes lit on two framed photos placed in a prominent spot, front and center, on the desk. I stepped around, curious to have a look.

I picked the one closest, with four people in the picture. They were outdoors, standing in front of large imposing rocks the color of rust red. The couple was on the left. The woman on the end, the boy between her and the man. To the right, another man stood, close enough for a group picture of everyone gathered together for the camera, but off to one side a bit, leaving a space between what was clearly a family unit of three. I could see a resemblance between the two men. The younger man was shorter and dashingly handsome, with a brash look. The older, dignified-looking man had his arm around the boy's shoulder.

I turned the frame around to Roth and pointed to the younger man. "Uncle Will?"

"That's him."

"The boy is unmistakably Bob," I said, recognizing him in the slight form of the child sandwiched between his parents. His father to his left, mother on the other side.

It captured a sliver in time, before tragedy had

struck. They seemed happy in that moment. The breeze had tousled the woman's loose long hair, lifting some strands that strayed across her cheek. She had lifted her chin and laughed, lips parted. The man on the right had turned his head to look in her direction. Maybe he'd heard her laughter and glanced at her. The picture was a spontaneous moment. I felt intrusive, like an outsider observing, knowing what they didn't know then—that their lives would be shattered soon. I set the photo gently on the desk and picked up the second one.

This one was more recent. I recognized the inn. A saddled horse was tied to the hitching post. Bob was sporting a wide grin, his hand resting on the saddle, as if he had just ridden. He had grown and was about a foot taller than he was in the other picture. Next to him, Will was looking at Bob with unmistakable affection and some pride. Comfortable and familiar. A family unit of two.

"Do you remember this?" I asked.

"Oh yeah." Roth laughed. "It was shortly after I'd started working here. I remember that day. Will had handed me his camera and asked me to take the photo."

"Are you a photographer?"

"No," he said. "I was so nervous, I almost dropped it. But it got them laughing. I told them to look at each other and quickly snapped a picture." He shook his head solemnly. "There's not a day that goes by when I don't look at it and think about that day. How happy they were."

"We need to talk," I said, quietly. "Like I mentioned, there's been a death. A guest at the inn this morning who checked out. The officers from the sheriff's office are here, upstairs, as we speak."

Roth was quiet. Perhaps he was taking in the new information. Or maybe he was still grappling with Will's death and mired in his sorrow.

"Did you not hear the commotion when they arrived?" I wanted to shake him.

"Someone assaulted this man at the park, across the street. I don't know when it happened or who discovered him, but Bob and I just left the scene a short while ago."

I tried again. "He stayed here two nights."

Roth was silent.

"Look, this man was probably in his forties or fifties. He has a shock of hair, but it's turning gray at the temples. Did you talk to him?"

"I'm not sure."

"Try to remember. Maybe you saw him or ran into him? Anything you can tell me." I was getting desperate. We didn't have a timeline, but if he saw Jack leaving this morning or sometime today, it'd give us a ballpark to work with.

"Like I said, I'm busy during tax season. I don't pay attention to trivial matters, who's coming and going."

I didn't appreciate his uppity attitude and the bit about trivial matters. From the way he acted, I almost expected him to charge me for the time. I was certain he didn't interact like this with Uncle Will. But he had an air of being in charge now, taking over Will's desk and getting paperwork for the taxes.

"Murder isn't trivial, *sir*," I said. "If you think of anything, call me." I wrote my cell phone number on a notepad, gave it to him, and walked out of the room.

CHAPTER THIRTY-THREE

I heard voices drifting from the dining area as I headed toward the coffee station for my dose of caffeine. It was later in the day, but I drank coffee at all hours. Even if I had it at midnight, it wouldn't keep me awake.

I hoped to catch Luna or Scarlett Bell. It was more likely to be other guests congregated around the refreshment station for their coffee, tea, or the snack of the day. I had sampled yesterday's plate of homemade cookies more than once. They were that good. It'd be a different treat each day of the week.

There were three people in the dining room. Luna, a guest I'd seen before, and a new face, presumably our latest guest.

Luna carried a plate of dark chocolate cookies and set it on the counter next to the coffeepot. She was talking to the new arrival, explaining it was self-serve for the two beverages—coffee or tea. The hot-water carafe and a tray of tea bags were on the other side of the coffee.

The other guest had a steaming mug in one hand and a generous-sized cookie in her other. She was matronly and probably around my mother's age. I recognized this woman from yesterday and walked up to her.

"I'll take that," I said, smiling as I pretended to snatch the cookie.

She laughed. "It just came out of the oven. Hon, get you a piece while it's still warm."

I liked her immediately upon hearing her little Southern accent and her bubbly laughter.

"Chocolate, yum," I said.

She was eyeing the dining room and the empty chairs lining the sides of the table. "Come join me."

"Okay," I said, dropping my cookie onto a plate and filling my mug.

The woman waited for me before eating. It reminded me of my mother and the good manners she had taught me. She patted the chair next to her, and I sat down.

"My name is Eve, by the way." I added a smile to my greeting.

"You can call me Mrs. Barnes," she said. "This is your first time here?"

I nodded with enthusiasm. "I'm on spring break. Midway College. And you?"

"I'm on my way to see my daughter in California.

Stopped here, as I've always wanted to see the Wild West."

"Me too," I said, taking a bite of my cookie. "And here we are enjoying the best homemade dark chocolate cookies with walnuts."

I waited until I swallowed my mouthful. "Would you mind if I asked you some questions? I'm curious by nature and a journalism student."

"You can practice on me," she said, laughing.

"Oh thanks," I said. "So, when did you arrive in town?"

"Yesterday. I checked in and got settled. Then I took a nap and fell asleep for about an hour."

"Did something wake you?"

"Yes, my alarm clock. I freshened up and brushed my hair and came downstairs."

"Why?"

"I had seen the sign for the afternoon refreshments. I got here a bit early and checked in, since my room was ready. Helped myself to some coffee and cookies."

"Did you know if someone was in the office?"

She shrugged. "I came straight here."

"For the treat."

"Yeah, and it was worth it."

I stared at my plate, a few crumbs scattered forlornly. "Perhaps you saw a certain man in his forties or fifties?"

"There was a man who opened the door for me on my way in. I'd say around that age."

"Yesterday or today?"

"Yesterday. When I was struggling to punch in my code because of my luggage. But before I could pull the door open, it swung open from the inside and this man almost ran into me."

"Did he introduce himself?" Maybe this was Jack.

"He was in a hurry. Murmured an apology and was out in the street before I could respond."

The clump of steps coming down the stairway interrupted our conversation. I saw Deputy Dillon in the lead and Bragg and Bob in the back.

"There's been a murder in the park," I whispered in Mrs. Barnes's ear. "He was a guest here, a man in his forties or fifties."

She gasped.

CHAPTER THIRTY-FOUR

Bob pulled me aside as the police talked to Luna and the two guests in the dining room.

"So what's happening next?" I asked.

"I gave him the contact info for the staff and guests. They'll be interviewing everyone here."

"Is Mrs. Bell gone?"

"I think she's long gone, but I didn't actually see her. When we checked Jack's room, we found the door locked. She had a light load this morning. Jack was the only guest who checked out."

"What about the handyman-maintenance guy? I haven't seen him around."

"He's finished his checklist. Only had a couple of things. Uncle Will is usually the one who does his work orders."

I squeezed Bob's arm and gave him a moment of silence before speaking again. "Oh, I just met your accountant."

"In Uncle Will's office?"

"You said he worked there, right?"

Bob relaxed like he'd just remembered. He nodded. He was probably so wound up he couldn't think straight.

"You were up there a good while with Deputy Dillon," I said.

His shoulders dropped—like his spirit. "He had a lot of questions."

"Because Jack was Uncle's Will's close friend," I said. "And because your uncle called and asked him for help?"

"He wasn't just my uncle's friend. He was a family friend. My friend, too."

"You told that to the deputies?"

"I told them about the past, going back to when I was little, after my parents died."

"I get it. He was a friend to all of you. Your close-knit family."

"He was there when I lost my parents." Bob's voice quaked and trembled. "When I became an orphan and Uncle Will leaned on him."

"But later, didn't you say he left?"

"He did. But like I said, I didn't know the reason. I was too young."

"Weren't you curious?"

He shrugged.

"I'm sorry."

He gritted his teeth. "I've lost my entire family. And now, Jack."

I was silent. Why did someone kill Jack? Was there a link to Uncle Will's death? I needed to think about how to proceed. A murderer might be in our midst.

A thought flashed. One that gave me the chills.

"Bob," I said, fighting the shaking in my voice. "We need to do everything we can to find the killer."

"Let the sheriff handle this."

I detected sadness and a touch of resignation as he said it. And shock. He was in no position to take charge. His face gave it up. I couldn't blame him. Nor could I force him to act and help solve this.

"Listen to me." I clenched my teeth. "We know who's the victim, but we don't know who killed him or why he was killed. Was the attack personal? Someone Jack knew? Or was it a crime committed by a total stranger?"

"The deputy said they haven't found a witness. Apparently, nobody saw the assault when it happened in the park."

"Don't you want to know why it happened?"

Bob said. "I can't do it now."

"I'm sorry if you think I'm pressing you. I don't have a right to do that. And I'm not judging you."

He didn't reply.

"This was a murder. We don't know if it was a random act by a stranger." I locked eyes with him and held it steadfast. "What if ... what if you're next?"

CHAPTER THIRTY-FIVE

Bob and I arrived early for dinner and seated ourselves at the small dining room table. The place settings and napkins were already in place like before, one per seat for each registered guest who made dinner reservations.

I was starved and tired, thankful we could stay at the inn for another home-cooked meal. The deputies had interviewed everyone, including me, before they left to survey the area and check out other witnesses and look for evidence.

The deputies later found out there was only one security camera at the inn, and it was outside at the front entrance. They had gone to check the footage and retrieve the video images. But when they got to it, they found out the system wasn't turned on, and it needed a reboot.

"Too bad the camera didn't capture anything," I said,

running my finger over the smooth surface of the napkin ring carved from horn. "Unfortunately, we don't have surveillance evidence of Jack Holt leaving the inn."

"It's a critical piece that's missing," Bob said.

I waved toward the street. "Surely there are other establishments with cameras?"

"Deputy Dillon said they'll be checking businesses around the inn, and those with cameras within a certain distance of the park."

"If they find a lot of cameras, it'll be hours of videos to review."

"Tedious work, if you ask me," Bob said. "I wouldn't want that job. My hat's off to whoever gets to do it."

"Man, they're going to be stretched thin. If they aren't already."

"I think Deputy Dillon was sorely disappointed our camera wasn't working. And frustrated. I got the impression maybe he blamed me at first." Bob heaved a sigh.

"It's unfair," I muttered. "He's in a tight spot. I'm not defending him, but he probably didn't mean to blame you. It wasn't your responsibility."

"Plenty of folks will pressure the sheriff's office for quick results. This being a tourist town. Anything that threatens their business and livelihood."

"Bad news travels fast."

"Good thing Roth was here to explain to them that Uncle Will was the person responsible for the security camera and rotating out hard drives or switching out the SD card when it was full."

"So that's who did it."

"After Will passed, the security camera routine fell through the cracks. Wasn't on his radar."

"Roth was busy working on the taxes when I talked to him. I can understand why he had his hands full," I said. "But Will's death affected everyone here. The camera wasn't on anyone's radar until the sheriff's department asked for the surveillance video."

"We had to talk Uncle Will into the camera in the first place. He fought us."

"Us?"

"Roth and me. We saw it differently. It's not a generational thing. My uncle was a fervent preservationist. He kept the exterior architecturally as close to the original as possible. Spoke strongly against the addition of cameras. Its intrusion. Ruins the facade."

I glanced toward the front door. "He compromised?"

"We came to an agreement. No camera inside. One camera outside by the front door. No camera in the back."

I paused as someone approached our table.

"Would you like your dinner now?" Luna was standing in front of us, carrying two plates.

I smiled. "Thank you."

"Yes, please," Bob said.

We had ordered our dinner ahead. The feature of the day was chili. The choice was beef or vegetarian.

She set our plated entrees down. A hefty bowl filled with thick chili with chunks of beef, tomatoes, beans, and corn for Bob, and a similar serving of meatless chili for me.

I dug in, spooning a mouthful before Bob got a taste of his.

"It's delicious," I complimented Luna when she came back with two side salads and small plastic containers with the dressing we had each chosen.

She grinned. "It's one of our favorites."

I wiped off a drizzle before it slid down my chin. "Thank you." I cleared my throat. "The man murdered today … Jack Holt. Did you happen to see when he checked out?"

"I couldn't say."

"You were preparing breakfast?"

"And cleanup after that. Made a shopping list."

"Did you go out?"

She chuckled. "Yeah, after I made the list."

"At what time do you think you were done?"

"Were?" Her voice lowered. "I'm still working now."

I could sympathize. "You work these long hours year-round?"

She shook her head. "Oh no. Only late fall and winter. This month will be our last for a while. We don't do dine-in dinners in the spring, summer, and early fall. It gives the guests more time to enjoy the beautiful outdoors. Then we start back again when the weather gets cold."

"That makes sense."

"It was Uncle Will's idea," Bob said. "A home away from home. The comfort of a bed and delicious, hearty home-cooked meals for weary travelers escaping the wintry storms raging outside."

We paused in a moment of silence, each lost in our thoughts.

CHAPTER THIRTY-SIX

I dreamt about Uncle Will last night. Flashes of visions, glimpses of the photos I'd seen in his office, on his desk. The faces up close, one after the other. Intense, then fading. A young man alone, then a child appeared by his side. The steadfast, fierce gaze of gray-blue eyes. The years fast-forwarded as his hair grayed and thinned, muscled arms and bulked chest lost their weight and girth. Yet his eyes held their strong gaze. The defiant eyes of a survivor. Of a man who had endured hardships and pain. Of a man who had suffered.

I tossed and turned, whipping my body in a frenzy and tangling the sheets. I saw his face, his mouth open and moving. Maybe he was crying out to me. Yet his screams were silent. Time and again he came to me, mouth open and twisting and gasping. Then the images became weaker and faded. Finally, a dullness appeared in his eyes, covering them like a film until their steely-blue color was obliterated.

I reached out, but he was no longer there. I woke up in a cold sweat. I kicked the cover off my bed.

The dream seemed so real. But it was also like a silent film. There were no speaking parts. The same scene with endless retakes, over and over. I couldn't hear a word. I could only watch.

I felt the urge to scream at him, "Tell me! I can't read your mind."

I was frustrated in reality, and in my dreams. What secrets were you hiding, Uncle Will?

A knock on my door startled me, followed by a loud call. "Housekeeping."

I realized I'd forgotten to hang the "Do Not Disturb" sign on the doorknob last night. I sighed and slid off the bed. My body weary and slow to react, my bare foot hit the cold floor. My body craved caffeine to recharge me. Coffee and breakfast were powerful motivators. A glance at the clock radio on the side table showed it was 9:32. I threw on my jeans and pulled a T-shirt over my head.

Mrs. Bell called out a second time and then let herself in. She looked surprised to see me, but quickly recovered.

I raised my hands, stretching my arms, and yawned.

"I can come back," she said.

"No, I'll get out of your way." I gathered my purse and walked toward the door. She turned aside to let me by.

I paused. "Scarlett, a man who was a guest here yesterday was killed in the park."

She blinked.

"His name was Jack Holt. Did you know him?"

She pushed her hair back. "I saw his name. I know the guests here."

"Right," I said. "Would you happen to know when he checked out?"

"I couldn't say."

"Bob and I are looking for information as to his whereabouts and timeline yesterday. Anything you can remember may help us," I said with an encouraging smile.

"I didn't see him yesterday morning," Scarlett said.

"Let me know If you remember anything else about our guest Jack."

CHAPTER THIRTY-SEVEN

Bob had texted me to meet him downstairs.

"The attorney called," he told me as I reached him.

"What did he say?" I asked.

"He wanted me to stop by and pick something up."

"What is it?"

"Something Uncle Will left for me."

"That's odd. Why didn't he give it to you before, when you went to his office?"

"I'll find out soon enough."

It was a brisk walk to the attorney's office. When we got there, Bob asked me to go in with him.

The place was clearly a one-man shop, with a small waiting area and an inner office. The attorney's name, James Garrett, was boldly embossed on the glass pane of his door. The receptionist smiled when we entered. Then she buzzed him.

"He's expecting you," she said. "You can go in."

"Thank you," Bob said.

As we walked in, his chair swiveled in our direction to reveal a heavyset, hefty-looking guy wearing a cowboy hat. I got the impression he was a tall fellow and once had the tight muscles of a young man.

"This is Eve Sawyer," Bob said. "My friend from Midway College."

"James Garrett." He bared his teeth in a smile.

"Nice to meet you," I said.

He gestured to the two empty chairs facing his desk and waited for us to sit.

"You're probably wondering why I asked you to come, so I'll get to the point."

Bob and I looked at each other.

"The man who was killed yesterday in the park was Jack Holt. He was a friend of Will Harding." Garrett fixed his gaze on Bob. "Before your uncle died, he came to see me."

Bob shifted in his chair. "Why?"

The attorney took his time. "This is a delicate matter," Garrett said. "Your uncle gave very explicit instructions. He planned for Jack Holt to come here so he could discuss this with him in person. However, Will made alternate arrangements in the event of his death, in which case Jack would relay his message to you directly. But with the untimely passing of Jack yesterday, that all changed."

Silence in the room. I glanced at Bob again and thought his face had turned pale.

Garrett opened a drawer, pulled out a folder, and

extracted a business envelope. "Your uncle would like you to have this."

Bob took the envelope addressed in Will's familiar handwriting. He flipped it over and saw that it was sealed. "What's this?"

"I'm not privy to its contents," Garrett said. "I'm just the messenger. But I do know it's a letter."

"Did my uncle discuss this with you?"

"No. I simply followed your uncle's wishes. I'm sorry. I don't know any more to tell you."

"Thank you," Bob said, rising.

"Oh, before you go …" Garrett leafed through the papers in the file folder.

Bob sat back down.

The attorney extracted a sheet of paper and placed it carefully on the desk in front of Bob. "Please take a look at this."

"What?" Bob leaned forward and studied it. "It's Uncle Will's bank statement."

"Yes, the monthly statement. As the executor, I have access to his bank accounts." The attorney pointed. "Now look on the account activity about halfway down the page, on the debits column.

"What am I looking for?"

"You'll see it."

I crossed my arms and turned my face away, giving Bob his privacy.

I heard the quick intake of his breath. I looked back.

He raised his head, a dazed look on his face.

"It's ... it's a large withdrawal." He tapped his finger on the amount.

"Do you know anything about this? It was a cash withdrawal, not a check."

Bob shook his head. "No, he didn't mention anything to me."

"Did he make a purchase? Make repairs to the house?" Garrett asked.

"I didn't see anything new or big changes to the house," Bob said. "But it does seem odd to withdraw so much cash."

We left the attorney's office. Bob was not in a talkative mood and we walked in silence back to the inn, stopping in front of the hitching post.

"Let's go in," he said, gesturing to the letter in his hand.

I wasn't ready to go in.

"I need to put this letter in my room." He noticed I hadn't budged.

"You do that," I said. "I'll be waiting outside."

CHAPTER THIRTY-EIGHT

I stood in front of the inn, waiting for Bob, but I was also tempted to leave him alone and go off on my own. That's when Serena stepped out the door, looking stylish in a pair of red wedges and a white lace-trim top and dark skinny jeans.

I called out to her.

She spotted me and walked over.

"Hey, look at you," I said, admiring her outfit. A pair of chunky earrings and a silver bracelet complemented her casual chic ensemble.

She blushed and fidgeted with her earring.

I caught sight of a flash of silver on her wrist. "Wait, is that the bracelet you were clutching the other day when you were fighting with your mother?"

"Oh that? Yes."

"Can I see it?"

She extended her arm, adjusting the bracelet so the front faced me.

I had never seen anything like it. It was a custom piece.

"What's on the back?" I asked.

She flipped it over.

It was engraved. I held it at an angle and made out the lettering, SB, but the next two initials were dull and faded, although the last letter looked like an H. "It's your mother's, right?"

"Yeah, but it's mine now," Serena reminded me.

"It's pretty," I said. "Do you know what the second set of initials stand for?"

"I asked her once, but she was evasive. When I pressed her, she wouldn't say who, but said it was given to her a long time ago by her boyfriend."

"So what happened to them?"

She shrugged, clearly losing interest in this conversation.

It was at that moment that Bob came back out.

"Hi, Serena," he said. "Oh, I just found out you worked yesterday. Thanks for helping out."

"My mom asked me to at the last moment. I didn't have a lot to do."

This was news to me. "Serena, you know what happened yesterday? Jack Holt, one of our guests, was murdered."

She nodded, averting her eyes.

"I just talked to your mom this morning and asked her. She said she didn't see him yesterday. So she wasn't working?"

"No, I was."

"Did she tell you why she took the day off?"

"No."

"The man who died—did you know Jack?"

Serena didn't speak.

I lowered my voice. "Let me rephrase it. Yesterday, did you happen to see or speak to Jack?"

Her lips trembled, and it looked like she was about to cry.

"I did what I was told."

I stared at her. "You did what?"

"I ... I gave him a message."

"What message, Serena?"

"To meet ... in the park."

"Who gave you the message?" My heart was pounding.

"My mother."

I snuck a peek at Bob, and his face was ashen. "So that's why Jack went to the park."

Serena licked her lips. "But she didn't go. I asked her later, after what happened."

"Why didn't she go?"

"She said she changed her mind."

CHAPTER THIRTY-NINE

"Let's get some ice cream," I said after Serena left. The nearby store touted homemade mouthwatering flavors and a choice of waffle or sugar cones.

Ice cream was my go-to comfort food. I remembered the times when I ate a whole carton right out of the box. Sometimes I'd scoop it out in the largest bowl as I could find. It didn't make the problem go away, but it made me feel better, at least for the time being, and took my mind off whatever was making me sad or bothering me. It was comforting and gave my taste buds a treat. I didn't know if ice cream would work for Bob, but I thought it was worth a try since I didn't have a magic pill.

He turned toward me, a vacant look on his face.

I tugged his arm gently. "Let's go in and sit."

Bob opened and closed his mouth, as if he was having a hard time making the decision.

"How about chocolate chip or caramel fudge?" I

asked. This time, without waiting for his answer, I steered him inside the store. I even sweetened the deal. "My treat."

The store was clean, neat, and sparkling with a newness that shouted, "Grand opening." The friendly staff bustled, oozing excitement. I glanced at the customers. A family occupied the center round table with a small energetic child who couldn't sit still. A young couple, oblivious to the world and their melting ice cream cones, shared the corner table, smiling and giggling like they were in love. A woman sat alone, occupying a window seat, comfortably settled in and absorbed in the pages of a romance novel.

We got our orders and took our seats at a quiet table in the back. Bob had the chocolate cheesecake. I got the french vanilla with a pinch of sea salt, which the ice cream store clerk had urged me to try. We ate in peace and quiet, enjoying our delicious treats, absorbed in our thoughts.

I finished first, and I let my gaze wander around the cute shop, then stopped—that's when I noticed the mounted camera on the corner wall. And it wasn't only one. There was another camera on the opposite corner of the room.

I waved to the staff and a woman came over right away like she was eager to address any problems I had.

"Excuse me," I said.

"How can I help you?" Her name tag read, "Manager Rachel Bennett."

"Do you have a surveillance camera outside?"

She stared at me. Said nothing.

"We're from Prospect Inn, a couple doors down. The man who was murdered at the park was a guest at the inn," I said.

Bob caught on quick with where I was going. "Ma'am, the sheriff's office tried to access our surveillance video, but unfortunately our security camera isn't working," he said. "My uncle didn't have a chance to fix it before he died."

"He was William Harding, the mayor, right?" she asked, her head bobbing with rapid nods.

"Yes," Bob said, leaning forward with a smile. "It would really help if we can take a look at your camera footage."

"Right now?"

"Yes please."

"That would suit. The sheriff's office has asked for the footage. I need to get my hands on it anyway."

Rachel led us to the back office to view the video. She gestured to two empty chairs for us to sit, then she sat down in front of the monitor and worked the controls. We gave her yesterday's date and a starting time, at approximately ten in the morning, then worked our way forward. It turned out they had pretty good image quality with this new camera. Although it wasn't aimed at the entrance to the inn, it had a wide view and captured people's faces at an odd angle, coming and going to and from the inn.

At first we went very slow, afraid of missing

anything. After about twenty or thirty minutes, she started fast forwarding the footage.

"Getting tired? I can take a turn," Bob offered.

"No, I'm fine," Rachel said.

"The offer is out there in case you change your mind."

She laughed.

I kept my eyes fixed on the screen while they chatted, getting the hang of it after a while. I saw a quick blur of blue flash by but didn't think anything of it at first. Then some blurry movement across the street.

"Wait," I said. "Can you wind it back a bit please and play it slow?"

She rewinded and then pressed the Play button.

I focused on the inn entrance and watched as a man wearing a blue plaid shirt and jeans came into view, his face partially obscured by the camera angle as he left the inn.

"Hold it!" I jumped up in my seat and made a note, jotting down the time on the video recording.

"That looks like Jack Holt," I heard Bob say.

"Can you go frame by frame?" I asked.

Then about a half minute later, another figure emerged from the inn. A tall man wearing a dark T-shirt and jeans, hair tied in a ponytail, face also partially obscured.

I watched the man as he walked behind Jack, moving to the intersection closer to the ice cream parlor, and crossed the street toward the park.

I turned to Rachel. "How about getting a closer look at this guy? Can you maybe zoom in on the face?"

She couldn't find a great angle for his face, but she got the best view she could and put it on the screen.

He was a good-looking guy. I'd say probably around forty.

I glanced at Bob and saw his eyes widen.

CHAPTER FORTY

I was in shock after seeing the surveillance footage—we all were, Bob, Rachel, and I.

Bob had identified the man as Tommy Carlson, the handyman/maintenance guy.

I called the sheriff's office and talked to Deputy Dillon. He asked me to snap a quick photo of the man and text it to him while he was waiting for Rachel to send the video footage.

A faint musty smell greeted us when we got back to the inn. Bob punched in the code, opening the door and allowing a ray of sunlight to shoot a weak beam on the beaten and weathered wood floor and ushering in a breath of fresh air, whipping a gust of dancing dust particles.

The inn was eerily quiet, undisturbed by the recent discovery of violence and crime outside.

"Is this an unusual occurrence?" I asked.

"If you're talking about major crime, I'd say so."

"I thought the tourist boom has revitalized this town, like other small towns in the West."

"This town has its place in history."

"Because it was a mining town?"

"Partly. The lore of the famous gunslinger and the outlaws made its mark here. Add the gold, the greed, the lawlessness, and it's the wild, wild west."

"And the miners."

"This place has seen more than its share of fights and drunken brawls."

"If only the walls had ears. The stories they'd tell," I said.

"If folks lived to tell it," Bob said. "Lives were short, and luck could be fleeting. People got killed for less than a penny, and some didn't have a reason."

"That certainly isn't fair."

"Who says life had to be fair? You lived each day, and beat it only to do it again another day. If a bullet or knife didn't find you, starvation, winter, illness, or childbirth would."

"It took a certain person to survive in the Wild West." I headed toward the stairs.

"Wait, I have to go into the office." Bob went down the hallway and disappeared.

I stayed on the stairs for a moment before bounding up the steps to my room. I needed to use the bathroom and refresh myself. At my door, I fumbled in my purse to find my key, then dropped it. Stooping down to pick it up, I noticed the sliver of light from the slightly open door. A chill ran down my spine. Thoughts ran through my mind. I tried to recall my steps when I left earlier. *Had I locked my door?* I went through the motions to jiggle my memory. Sometimes things that were routine became so automatic, I didn't even think about it. My hand shook as I reached for the doorknob, more certain than not that I'd remembered to lock it. *But then who opened my door? How did they get in? Why were they in my room?*

I jumped at the sound of shoes clumping up the stairs. Relief and worry must have washed over my face upon seeing Bob. "Oh, there you are," I said.

He noticed. "What's wrong?"

"I'm sure I locked my door."

He looked at the key in my hand and the door. "I'm going in first." He gestured for me to stay back, pushed open the door, and stepped across the doorway. He stood there, scanning my room, then briskly walked across to check the bathroom and the closet before signaling me to come inside.

I was still spooked. I walked to the bed, whisked the covers back, and looked under the bed and behind it.

"Satisfied?" Bob asked.

"Wait," I said.

I pulled open the dresser drawers. My neatly folded clothes and socks had been tossed around. "There's my answer. Somebody was definitely in my room." I shivered. "They went through my stuff. Whoever it was made no attempt to hide it."

"Anything missing?"

"Won't know for sure until I go over everything." I chewed my lip, thinking about the items I'd packed for this trip. I traveled light, and I carried my phone, money, and purse with me. A quick check told me nothing had been taken. "All there."

Maybe they weren't looking for something from me. "Let's check your room," I said to Bob, concerned.

His face paled. Bob hurried to his room.

"Oh my God," he shouted.

I rushed after him.

His stuff was tossed all over. On the chair, table, bed, floor. He'd packed a large suitcase, stuffed it to the brim, bringing a lot more than I did.

I gasped involuntarily as it dawned on me that Bob *was* the target. Whoever it was took a big risk coming in our rooms, not knowing which was his and when we'd be back. We could have walked in on that person.

I took a step back, skirting the items on the floor. "Do you need my help?" I offered, even though I didn't know how much help I could be, being clueless as to what would be missing or not.

"No, I know what to look for," Bob said grimly.

"I'll check the other rooms," I said. "Maybe we aren't the only targets."

CHAPTER FORTY-ONE

I thought about Will Harding as I walked down the hallway to check the lock on the guest room adjoining mine. The check-in at the inn had been self-serve. When guests arrived, they were greeted by a table in the front room, a welcome sign on a silver tray, and a basket holding envelopes stamped with an embossed logo of Prospect Inn and the handwritten name of the guest on the front. Inside each envelope was a printed welcome note and the key to the room.

Bob and I weren't technically guests at the inn, but we were given the same treatment. He explained this to me beforehand, how the process worked when he registered us online and entered a special code. We didn't have to pay a deposit and the charges on our invoices would have a balance of zero. But we were counted as guests because it had something to do with the accounting and the workload of the staff as well as the planning for the meals that were included in our stay.

A day before our arrival, we'd received a code for the front door. It was a four-digit number we'd punch in, which would then release the lock and let us inside.

The whole process was seamless. Up to that point, we hadn't met a single soul. Bob explained if Uncle Will were alive, we'd have met him. He was very much the presence and essence of the place, and he personally liked to greet each guest when schedules allowed. His demise left a gaping hole in the place, depriving the guests of a warm personal welcome.

I jiggled and turned the knob. It was locked. I continued to check the other doors down the hallway. No door was open.

"Hey," Bob shouted.

I heard him from across the hall. I quickly made my way down to his room. "What's up?"

Bob was standing by the table, arms outstretched. One hand held the open shoebox, the other hand, the lid. His hands were shaking. He didn't speak.

"Something is missing?"

He nodded, taking a few steps closer to me.

I looked inside. "If you're asking me what's missing, I couldn't say."

Bob gave a vigorous shake of his head. "I put it there."

"Okay, I can't read your mind. You're going to have to be more specific."

"The letter is missing," he said.

"Was it in the shoebox the other day?" I had caught a glimpse of the contents the other day but didn't recall seeing a letter, although there were only a few items at the top.

"No."

"Then how do you know it's missing?"

"Because I put it there," Bob said. "On top."

I tried to remain calm. Bob was rattled and visibly upset.

"You put the letter from the attorney in the shoebox?"

He nodded.

"Well ... did you open it?"

"No, not yet. I was going to do it later. Saving it for the right time to go through the contents of the box."

"You have no idea what's in the letter," I said, keeping the disappointment out of my voice.

Bob sat back down in the chair, his shoulders slumped.

I bit my lip. I had no right to judge him or blame him. He asked for my support, and I'd failed him. Moreover, he was shaken by the attack in the park and Jack's death. I tried again. "I'm sorry," I said. "I had no right."

He blinked in acknowledgement.

I put my hand on his arm and gave a reassuring squeeze. "I'm sorry about Jack too. Whoever did that in the park ... Whoever did this probably knew both Jack and your uncle."

"Maybe that person was also looking for something

in our rooms," Bob said. "I booked both rooms under my name, and when they didn't find it in your room first, they searched for it in mine."

"And found it, your letter."

"This is scary. Whoever it is had to have been pretty sure that either you or I had this letter."

"Which may put us in danger, possibly."

We became silent. I had to think. A robber and a murderer might be in our midst.

"We need to call Deputy Dillon," I said, reaching for my cell. When he didn't pick up, I let it go to voicemail and left a message.

CHAPTER FORTY-TWO

I dreamt about Uncle Will again last night. Weird stuff. The camera on the front door of Prospect Inn dangling on a wire. Soaked by a heavy torrent of rain, water splashed on the lens, obscuring it. Wind gusts tossed and whipped the camera, banging it against the door, shattering it.

A flash of lightening lit up the sky, exposing the broken camera crashed on the pavement. Thunder boomed. People screamed. People ran into the park, the tree branches shaking and waving in the wind. More screaming. Cries for help. Darkness. I opened my eyes, but my vision was blurry.

I tossed and turned.

My heart raced. I flung my legs out, working them furiously as I ran. I heard Will's cries. "Faster, faster," he urged.

THE MORNING CAME. I woke up, feeling unrested. I reached for my phone to check the time. It was early, 6:53 a.m.

I jumped out of bed and went in the bathroom. Then I opened the curtains, letting the sunlight in the room. I felt better.

The days seemed to run into each other. I jerked my head back. What was today? Was I going back soon? I reached for my phone on the table and pulled up my itinerary.

Whew, I blew out a breath of relief. Two more days.

I could get ready to pack and return home. I thought about the murder of Jack Holt. The investigation of the case. The surveillance footage. The suspect.

Should I start packing? I glanced at the dresser drawers. I didn't have much. The clothes I brought with me.

I saw the souvenir gift I bought sitting on the table, still wrapped in newspapers. I smiled. My mother would like it, I was sure. I picked the item up, looking at it and turning it over, remembering how I found it in the general store. My eyes caught a partial headline and the words "Mayor" and "Dedication." I carefully removed the tape and unwrapped the newspaper, flattening the crinkles and smoothing the edges on the table.

I read the full article, enjoying it more now that I

had the context. The story was above the fold; a large photo front and center showed a smiling William Harding at the dedication of the park in his honor. I leaned in to study his face, older and more salt than pepper in his hair than I'd seen in previous photos, but clearly it was the same man, still looking distinguished and handsome. The photo caption identified his name and the place and date. Underneath, the photographer's name was credited.

It was a good picture. A second, smaller side photo was taken from another angle and showed the people at the dedication and their smiling faces. I took a closer look to see if I recognized anyone else, half-expecting to see a familiar face—until I did. My hands trembling, I smoothed the paper more and blinked.

"Oh no, no!" I shouted. The face was partly turned away, but from the angle, it was unmistakable. It was the man with the ponytail—from the surveillance camera. Tommy Carlson.

His face was turned like he was talking or smiling with someone. I couldn't see who, as it was cut off from the photo.

I heard a knock on the door. "Hey, Eve, are you okay?" Bob said. He'd heard me.

I ran to open the door. "You've got to see this!"

"Whoa, what's happening?" he said, looking like he was puzzled and amused and curious.

"Come in." I shut the door and rushed back to the table and pointed to the picture.

He nodded and smiled broadly. "I know. Uncle Will's big day."

"No," I said, putting my finger right on the guy's neck. "Does he look familiar to you?"

It took about a second before Bob's mouth fell open. "Tommy …"

"Now look at the date and tell me when he was hired."

"He wasn't hired yet."

"It's him. It looks like he's with someone. I can't tell who," I said. Then a thought occurred to me. "Bob, do you know where the newspaper office is?"

"It's past the attorney's office, about another block."

"Let's go. We'll ask about the photo files for that article. Maybe we can find out who he's with."

"Okay."

Things were moving fast. "We don't have a second to waste," I said.

CHAPTER FORTY-THREE

The newspaper office was on the main floor of a small building.

"It publishes one day a week," Bob said.

"What day?"

"Wednesday."

"Does it have an online presence?"

"It does, but it's a small subscriber base, with the size of the town."

"Do people prefer the print newspaper?"

"Yes."

We opened the door and went in. There was a small reception area, an office near the front, and a corner office in the back.

The receptionist looked up with a pleasant smile. "Hello, how may I help you?"

"We'd like to see Doug Bennett," I said.

She glanced at the office with the glass door, which

she could see right through. He was at his desk. "What's this in regard to?"

"Will Harding," Bob said. "Doug was the photographer at my uncle's dedication ceremony in the park."

"Ah yes," she said, nodding. She dialed, spoke to Doug, and hung up. "He'll see you now."

"Thank you," Bob said.

We walked in his office, past the glass door with his name on it.

He rose up from his desk chair, smiling as he greeted us. "Doug."

"Bob Harding."

"And I'm Eve Sawyer."

We shook hands all around.

"You're visiting?" Doug asked, looking at me.

"Yes. First time out West." I flashed a grin. "Bob and I are here on spring break from Midway College."

He gave a nod. "I've heard of it. It's one of the best small colleges in the southeast."

Bob and I exchanged looks. "Yeah, I like it," he said.

"I went there to study journalism," I said.

"Please sit," Doug said. He waited until we were settled. "So, you're here about Will Harding's article?"

"Yes, I understand you took the photos at his dedication ceremony," I said, taking a quick peek in Bob's direction. "He was Bob's uncle."

Doug nodded.

"We'd like to know if you have other photos of the people there."

"I believe I took a few. I usually do. And pick out the best ones for the feature." He frowned. "Why do you ask?"

I met his gaze. In a moment of quick thinking, I snatched my phone and scrolled the photos until I found what I was looking for.

"Here," I said, holding my phone out, showing the picture I'd snapped of the man in the surveillance video.

He moved in, taking a closer look. I thought I saw surprise register on his face. "You met my wife, Rachel."

Now it was our turn to look surprised.

He touched the nameplate on his desk, specifically the last name, "Bennett."

It dawned on me. "You're married to Rachel Bennett, the manager of the ice cream store."

Doug laughed. "Small world. News travels fast." He got up and went to a file cabinet by the wall and searched. Wrote down a number, then went to another cabinet. "Our images are stored digitally, but sometimes we have a few prints also."

He came back with a small paper folder with prints and carefully spread them out on his desk.

Bob and I stood up and leaned over the photos to have a better look.

Doug sorted the photos and separated two from the rest. "Here, take a look at these."

Bob and I each picked up one.

Then we traded.

Our eyes met.

I checked again and scrutinized the face in the photo, then placed it back on the desk.

"It's her," I said.

CHAPTER FORTY-FOUR

There was no mistaking her. She was laughing, beaming. Like she was happy, or he'd said something amusing. His face was turned. Staring into her big, beautiful eyes. Like he was lovesick. Like the Bob Dylan song, "Love Sick."

Scarlett Bell.

I almost didn't recognize her—at first. Because I didn't see an angry, bitter woman.

This woman looked younger. Her face radiant.

Then I saw their hands were touching, like lovers.

It hit me then—the pieces coming together into focus, like the photo centering on Scarlett. She was the focal point. It all made sense now.

I picked up her picture, holding it up to Doug and Bob. "Scarlett Bell. She's at the heart of it all."

"What do you mean?" Doug said.

"Scarlett lured Jack to the park, through a message she asked her daughter to convey, which she did, as the unknowing person in this situation. But Scarlett didn't show up. The video footage from your wife's surveillance camera showed Jack leaving the inn, then Tommy," I said, tapping the screen of my cell phone. "He followed Jack as he crossed the street to the park."

"Jack was a guest at Prospect Inn. Scarlett is the housekeeper at our inn, and Tommy also works there as the handyman and maintenance guy," Bob said.

"So I think Tommy shows up instead and kills Jack," I said. "If Scarlett's daughter hadn't mentioned to us about the message to Jack, we wouldn't have connected the dots."

"You figured out the killer. Sounds like it was a setup, the two of them working in tandem," said Doug. "But my question is why?"

"Good question," I said. "We know that Jack came here when his close friend Will called him for help. But he died before Jack arrived. Jack didn't tell us what help Will asked for. Maybe Jack knew something that got him killed or he was in the way."

I raised my eyebrows in Bob's direction, not willing to betray any confidence of our meeting at his attorney's office. "I think money may also have something to do with it."

"I agree," Bob said. "We learned that Uncle Will had withdrawn a large sum of money in cash. Since it wasn't a check, there's no way to know who the money was for. But it was highly suspect and unusual."

"Gosh, maybe it was blackmail, *ergo* the cash," Doug said.

"And Bob just got robbed at the inn too," I said.

"You guys better be careful," Doug said. "The killers are still out there."

I whipped out my phone and punched the call button for Deputy Dillon.

CHAPTER FORTY-FIVE

Tommy Carlson dragged his weary body to the couch. Sank into its warm welcome. A sure thing he looked forward to every night. At home.

He eased his pain-wracked body into a comfortable spot. He was sick of it. The hard life. The struggles. The loneliness. But most of all, he was sick of *her*.

Scarlett. The curse and bane of his existence.

It started out bright enough. That day so long ago. She'd stood outside his auto repair shop. The blazing rays of sun outlined her firm, youthful, succulent body through the sheer fabric of her cotton dress. The gentle breeze played with the soft cloth, teasing it this way and that, wrapped it around and between her long slim legs. She'd called out to him when she spotted him changing tires on a four-door sedan on the rack.

Tommy turned his head. Saw her. And took a second look. That was when he was hooked.

It was all business at first. Scarlett was checking

prices for a repair on her old clunker. He sensed her question had rolled off her tongue like it'd been asked many times before. He gave her a low bid, one he was sure no other place could or would match. Her large, beautiful eyes widened like she was surprised. "How much?" she'd asked, making him repeat it.

He repeated the amount, slower this time. "It ... it's okay?" he managed to stutter.

It wasn't technically *his* shop—yet. But his old man had told Tommy it would be his one day. He was the older of the two children, senior by six years to his younger brother. So Tommy had assumed more responsibilities as time went on and taken over more of the reins and became the boss of the place, even before it was signed and deeded to him. The sweat dampened his armpits as he awaited for her decision. She took her time. Made him wait like she was playing with her prey.

When Scarlett finally said yes, his heart pounded and did a little flip.

Back then it was innocence and joking around. They fooled around some too. But she called the shots, putting a stop to things before he got too far. No one could blame him for trying. She was the prize. A beauty with class and brains. Truth be known, he would have waited as long as he could.

Then it all changed—the day Scarlett caught the eye of a young man who brought his fancy new car to the shop. His name was William Harding.

Tommy clenched his hand, digging nails into his roughened palm.

He'd called her and left messages. But she ghosted him.

It was a few months before he saw her again. One day she came to the shop while Tommy was working on a car. He looked up and saw her. But his didn't drop his tools and run to her. He let her wait on him.

Scarlett called out his name softly as if nothing wrong had happened between them. As if they could pick up their friendship. As if nothing—and no one—had ever come between them.

He felt a flutter rise in this stomach. He fought it, clenching his teeth and keeping his head down and concentrating on the work. When Tommy finished replacing the alternator, he slammed the hood down, harder than he needed, but seeing her flinch gave him some satisfaction.

She invited herself over to his place that night. A bottle of wine in one hand, and a large brown takeout bag in the other. He didn't have to ask what it was. He recognized the delicious scent of their favorite Chinese food. A familiar scent from a place he still kept on speed dial on his cell phone.

But something was different tonight. After dinner, Scarlett gave him a peace offering. Finally, Tommy got what he had dreamed and prayed for. That night he slept well, a smile stretched across his face as he wrapped his arms around his girl.

He had heard the words "fury, woman scorned"

strung together. He would soon find out what part he would play in Scarlett's revenge plan—the role of a mechanic that he was perfectly suited to play.

YEARS LATER, Scarlett had cajoled Tommy into moving. Leaving Ravine where he grew up. To Prospect. Tommy had resisted at first, reluctant to leave his successful auto shop business behind. But his younger brother had grown up and was eager to run the family business. They struck a deal. Tommy packed up his belongings and drove out of town with her.

Scarlett had found out Will lived in Prospect. He had prospered, becoming the mayor and the owner of the local inn. She'd surprised him. Called him up.

"Remember me?" she asked Will. "This is Scarlett."

Stunned silence greeted her ears.

"Where are you?" he sputtered.

"Right outside your door."

They met in his office. She had it all planned out. What she was going to say. She had also bought a new dress. Almost like the one she wore when they first met. A ploy to disarm him. But he'd forgotten her. He never suspected her revenge. He thought it was a friendly call.

Until it wasn't.

CHAPTER FORTY-SIX

Bob and I came back to Prospect Inn after our semester ended. It was summer. I faced the blistering heat, unlike the weather about two months ago.

We sat across the desk from Deputy Dillon—except he wasn't. The sheriff had retired with pomp and circumstance after the murders. He'd served for thirty years. The man facing us was now the new sheriff in town. Sheriff Dillon.

"Congratulations," I said at the same time as Bob.

The sheriff sported a wide grin. He looked handsome in his crisp uniform, and the sparkling new brass name tag did go well with it.

"You look great," Bob said, echoing my thoughts exactly.

He nodded and looked aside. I detected the faint blush coloring the cheeks of a man who was humble and not used to compliments.

"Thanks, but I ... I didn't call you in for this," he said, turning serious.

He held a folder in front of him. "We exhumed your uncle. An autopsy was conducted, and DNA and other samples were collected for testing." He opened the folder and flipped the pages.

I sneaked a peek at Bob. His lips were pursed. He looked tense, as if all the weight and worry about his uncle's death had descended again.

Dillon cleared his throat. "The results of the autopsy on William Harding showed cause of death was asphyxiation. And determined the manner of death to be homicide."

"Was he smothered by a pillow over his face while he was sleeping?" I asked.

"It's possible it was a pillow, or other means of suffocation."

"Who did the autopsy?"

"We contracted a forensic pathologist for this autopsy. He was present at the exhumation."

"From where?" I asked, wondering if was done in town or if the body had been transported elsewhere. "Where was it done?"

"Denver."

"Were you also present at the exhumation?"

"Yes."

"Have you done any exhumations before?"

"No, not me. Not this office. It's very rare. We sought an outside forensic pathologist, a medical doctor who had prior experience with exhumations and had performed autopsies on exhumed bodies."

"And he reached the conclusion of cause of death?"

"Yes," Dillon said, pressing his palm over the file. "It's in the report."

"And by homicide. How did he determine the manner of death?"

"There were bruises on both upper arms."

"Forcible holding or restraining ..." I said as the word *murder* came to mind. I had one more question. "Did the doctor find evidence of poisoning?"

"He didn't in the autopsy, as the toxicological investigations were inconclusive in the samples he collected."

CHAPTER FORTY-SEVEN

AFTER AN INTENSIVE AND EXTENSIVE INVESTIGATION, including interviews, an autopsy, test results, and the findings of evidence, the police arrested Scarlett Bell and Tommy Carlson on charges relating to the murders of William Harding and Jack Holt.

SCARLETT AND TOMMY'S relationship went way back, for years. They began as friends, although it didn't stay that way later. Then she met Will. He had money and he was handsome. They became involved. But he left her for Bob's mother, a married woman. Scarlett shook with rage and hurt. Her fury had no bounds. She sought vengeance.

She found Will Harding years later and blackmailed him, threatening to expose his dark secret about his illicit affair with Bob's mother—while she was married to his older brother. Will made the cash payment. But when Scarlett demanded more money later, he refused to pay again, so she started to poison him little by little. Not a large dose to risk him ending up in the hospital. Only a smaller dose to make him feel unwell. But Will was stronger than she realized and it was taking longer than she planned. In the end, his death came quick when she killed him with the help of Tommy, snuffed by his own pillowcase.

When Jack came sniffing around, they killed him before he spilled the secret. Jack had disapproved of the affair, and although he kept his promise to help Will after Bob's parents died, he later distanced himself from Will after he left Ravine.

Scarlett and Tommy came up with a new scheme to wait until after Bob inherited Will's money, then they'd blackmail Bob, gauging he would do anything to protect his mother's secret and his beloved uncle's legacy in Prospect.

EPILOGUE

James Garrett testified in the murder trial. When the prosecutor introduced the exhibit and showed Garrett an envelope in a plastic bag, he identified it as the item he had given to Bob, which was then moved into evidence. Tommy Carlson had followed Bob and me to Garrett's office. After Bob came back to Prospect Inn and dropped off the letter, Tommy went to search for it, ultimately stealing it. The motive was to get more information to use to blackmail Bob, after Will Harding died and he could no longer be blackmailed.

Serena, age fifteen and ten months, filed an emancipation petition with the court in Colorado with the help of James Garrett. She never knew who her father was. A paternity test was done and provided a match with Tommy Carlson. Serena eventually got the bracelet back—it had been taken as evidence when her mother revealed the giver's initials were WH, Will Harding.

After their arrest, she got a part-time job at Prospect Inn to support herself while she finished school. Bob had inherited the inn, and he covered Serena's salary and provided room and board. He arranged this with Mr. Roth, who agreed to run the inn while Bob was away in college.

DOUG BENNETT BROKE the story in the town's newspaper and shared the byline with me, giving me credit. He took the lead and sent me the initial draft for input. I wrote pieces of it, filled in gaps, and smoothed the story out. We collaborated and worked quickly to meet his paper's Wednesday deadline. He often multitasked as both the reporter and the photographer. Subsequent to our first article, Doug continued to cover the story by himself, garnering an increase in readership subscriptions. He was kept very busy with a series of articles following this story, which also increased traffic on their web page and got picked up by major newspapers and national evening news.

THE STOLEN letter was returned to Bob. Although Bob never divulged its contents, saying it was intensely personal and private, he did reveal that it was a letter written by his mother to William Harding, dated the day she died.

There was a note attached to it from Will that this letter was written the day she died and the last day they had met. It was delivered by the mailman a few days afterward.

He wrote to Bob: "When you get this, I will have died. Your mother was the great love of my life, but her death and the death of your father was my greatest sadness. I have lived with the guilt of what I've done, which was an immense dishonor and betrayal to my brother, your father. I lived my life under this darkness and shame. I hope you'll forgive me some day, but I have no right to ask anything from you. You have brought me love and joy. For that I'm eternally grateful."

The deaths and possible murders of Bob's parents had never been investigated. The remains of their car were junked and disposed of long ago.

OH, and I made it to Pikes Peak. Bob and I rented a car and we drove up the mountain, reaching the pinnacle —the summit. What could top that magnificent view?

ABOUT THE AUTHOR

Jane Suen is an award-winning author who writes mysteries, sci-fi thrillers, short stories, contemporary romance, and crime fiction.

While driving through Alabama on a hot summer afternoon, she saw a "Murder Creek" road sign which inspired her first book in the Eve Sawyer Mystery series. *Murder in Prospect* is her fifth book in the series.

SHORT STORIES

Beginnings and Endings: A Selection of Short Stories

I Ain't Afraid of Nothin'